Charles Battell Loomis

The Four-Masted Cat-Boat, and Other Truthful Tales

Charles Battell Loomis

The Four-Masted Cat-Boat, and Other Truthful Tales

ISBN/EAN: 9783337413156

Printed in Europe, USA, Canada, Australia, Japan

Cover: Foto ©Andreas Hilbeck / pixelio.de

More available books at **www.hansebooks.com**

The
Four-Masted Cat-Boat
And Other Truthful Tales

By
Charles Battell Loomis

**With illustrations by
Florence Scovel Shinn**

New York
The Century Co.
1899

THE DE VINNE PRESS.

TO MY BROTHER

HARVEY WORTHINGTON LOOMIS

I DEDICATE THIS COLLECTION

OF SKETCHES

C. B. L.

Preface

To send a book into the world without a preface is like thrusting a bashful man into a room full of company without introducing him; and there could be only one thing worse than that,—to a bashful man,—and that would be to introduce him.

In introducing my book to the reader (how like a book-agent that sounds!) I wish to say that the only bond of union between the various sketches is that they were all done by the same hand—or hands, as they were written on a typewriter.

Whether it would have added to their interest to have placed the same characters in each sketch is not for me to say, but it would have been a great bother to do it, and in getting up a book the thing to avoid is bother. It has n't bothered me to write it. I hope it won't bother you to read it, for I 'd hate to have you bothered on my account.

C. B. L.

Contents

A FEW IDIOTISMS

AT THE LITERARY COUNTER

CONTENTS

NOTE

I am indebted to the editors of the "Century," the "Saturday Evening Post," "Harper's Bazar," "Puck," the "Critic," the "Criterion," and the S. S. McClure Syndicate for permission to use the articles which first met printers' ink in their columns. C. B. L.

A FEW IDIOTISMS

I

THE FOUR-MASTED CAT-BOAT

AN ETCHING OF THE SEA, BY A LANDLUBBER

THE sea lay low in the offing, and as far as the eye could reach, immense white-caps rode upon it as quietly as pond-lilies on the bosom of a lake.

Fleecy clouds dotted the sky, and far off toward the horizon a full-rigged four-masted cat-boat lugged and luffed in the calm evening breezes. Her sails were piped to larboard, starboard, and port; and as she rolled steadily along in the heavy wash and undertow, her companion-light, already kindled, shed a delicate ray across the bay to where the dull red disk of the sun was dipping its colors.

Her cordage lay astern, in the neat coils that seamen know so well how to make. The anchor had been weighed this half-hour, and the figures put down in the log; for Captain Bliffton was not a man to put off doing anything that lay in the day's watch.

Away to eastward, two tiny black clouds stole along as if they were diffident strangers in the sky, and were anxious to be gone.   Now and again came the report of some sunset gun from the forts that lined the coast, and sea-robins flew with harsh cries athwart the sloop of fishing-boats that were beating to windward with gaffed topsails.

"Davy Jones 'll have a busy day to-morrow," growled Tom Bowsline, the first boatswain's mate.

"Meaning them clouds is windy?" answered the steward, with a glance to lee-ward.

"The same," answered the other, shaking out a reef, and preparing to batten the tarpaulins.   "What dinged fools them fellers on the sloop of fishin'-ships

is! They 've got their studdin'sails
gaffed and the mizzentops aft of the gang-
way; an' if I know a marlinspike from a
martingale, we 're goin' to have as pretty
a blow as ever came out of the south."

And, indeed, it did look to be flying in
the face of Providence, for the mackerel-
ships, to the last one, were tugging and
straining to catch the slightest zephyr,
with their yard-arms close-hauled and
their poop-decks flush with the fo'c'sle.

The form of the captain of the cat-boat
was now visible on the stairs leading to
the upper deck. It needed but one keen
glance in the direction of the black clouds
—no longer strangers, but now perfectly
at home and getting ugly—to determine
his course. "Unship the spinnaker-boom,
you dogs, and be quick about it! Luff,
you idiot, luff!" The boatswain's first
mate loved nothing better than to luff, and
he luffed; and the good ship, true to her
keel, bore away to northward, her back
scuppers oozing at every joint.

"That was ez neat a bit of seamanship
ez I ever see," said Tom Bowsline, taking

a huge bite of oakum. "Shiver my timbers! if my rivets don't tremble with joy when I see good work."

"Douse your gab, and man the taff-rail!" yelled the captain; and Tom flew to obey him. "Light the top-lights!"

A couple of sailors to whom the trick is a mere bagatelle run nimbly out on the stern-sprit and execute his order; and none too soon, for darkness is closing in over the face of the waters, and the clouds come on apace.

A rumble of thunder, followed by a

blinding flash, betokens that the squall is
at hand.   The captain springs adown the
poop, and in a hoarse voice yells out:
" Lower the maintop; loosen the shrouds;
luff a little—steady!   Cut the main-brace,
and clear away the halyards.   If we don't
look alive, we 'll look pretty durn dead
in two shakes of a capstan-bar.   All hands
abaft for a glass of grog."

The wild rush of sailors' feet, the creak-
ing of ropes, the curses of those in the
rear, together with the hoarse cries of the
gulls and the booming of the thunder,
made up a scene that beggars description.
Every trough of the sea was followed by
a crest as formidable, and the salt spray
had an indescribable brackish taste like
bilge-water and ginger-ale.

After the crew had finished their grog
they had time to look to starboard of the
port watch, and there they beheld what
filled them with pity.   The entire sloop
of mackerel-ships lay with their keels up.

" I knowed they 'd catch it if they
gaffed their studdin'sails," said Tom, as
he shifted the quid of oakum.

1*

The full moon rose suddenly at the exact spot where the sun had set. The thunder made off, muttering. The cat-boat, close-rigged from hand-rail to taff-rail, scudded under bare poles, with the churning motion peculiar to pinnaces, and the crew involuntarily broke into the chorus of that good old sea-song:

The wind blows fresh, and our scuppers are astern.

THE POOR WAS MAD

A FAIRY SHTORY FOR LITTLE
CHILDHER

ANCE upon a toime the poor was
virry poor indade, an' so they
wint to a rich leddy that was
that rich that she had goold finger-nails,
an' was that beautifil that it 'u'd mek you
dopey to luke at her. An' the poor asht
her would she give thim the parin's of her
goold finger-nails fer to sell. An' she
said she would that, an' that ivery
Chuesdeh she did be afther a-parin' her
nails. So of a Chuesdeh the poor kem an'
they tuke the goold parin's to a jewel-ery
man, an' he gev thim good money fer
thim. Was n't she the koind leddy,
childher? Well, wan day she forgot to

pare her nails, an' so they had nothin' to
sell.   An' the poor was mad, an' they wint
an' kilt the leddy intoirely.   An' whin she
was kilt, sorra bit would the nails grow
upon her, an' they saw they was silly to
kill her.   So they wint out to sairch fer a
leddy wid silver finger-nails.   An' they
found her, an' she was that beautifil that
her face was all the colors of the rainbow
an' two more besides.   An' the poor asht
her would she give thim the parin's of her
silver finger-nails fer to sell.   An' she said
that she would that, an' that ivery
Chuesdeh she did be afther a-parin' her
nails.   So of a Chuesdeh the poor kem an'
they tuke the silver parin's to the jewel-ery
man, an' he gev thim pretty good money
fer thim, but not nair as good as fer the
goold.   But he was the cute jewel-ery
man, was n't he, childher?   Well, wan day
she forgot to pare her nails, an' so they
had nothin' to sell.   An' the poor was
mad, an' they wint an' kilt the leddy intoirely.   An' whin she was kilt, sorra bit
would the nails grow upon her, an' they
saw they was silly to kill her.   So they

wint out to sairch for a leddy wid tin
finger-nails. An' they found her, an' she
was that beautifil that she would mek you
ristless. An' the poor asht her would she
give thim the parin's of her tin finger-nails
fer to sell. An' she said she would that,

an' that ivery Chuesdeh she did be afther
a-parin' her nails. So of a Chuesdeh the
poor kem. An' did they git the tin nails,
childher? Sure, that 's where y' are out.
They did not, fer the leddy had lost a
finger in a mowin'-machine, an' she did n't
have tin finger-nails at arl, at arl—only
noine.

III

A PECULIAR INDUSTRY

HE sign in front of the dingy little office on a side-street, through which I was walking, read:

JO COSE AND JOCK EWLAH
FUNSMITHS

Being of an inquisitive turn of mind, I went in. A little dried-up man, who introduced himself as Mr. Cose, greeted me cheerily. He said that Mr. Ewlah was out at lunch, but he 'd be pleased to do what he could for me.

"What is the nature of your calling?" asked I.

"It is you who are calling," said he, averting his eyes. Then he assumed the voice and manner of a "lecturer" in a

10

dime museum, and rattled along as follows:

"We are in the joke business. Original and second-hand jokes bought and sold. Old jokes made over as good as new. Good old stand-bys altered to suit the times. Jokes cleaned and made ready for the press. We do not press them ourselves. Joke expanders for sale cheap. Also patent padders for stories—"

I interrupted the flow of his talk to ask him if there was much demand for the padders.

"Young man," said he, "do you keep up with current literature?"

Then he went over to a shelf on which stood a long line of bottles of the size of cod-liver-oil bottles, and taking one down, he said: "Now, here is Jokoleine, of which we are the sole agents. This will make a poor joke salable, and is in pretty general use in the city, although some editors will not buy a joke that smells of it."

I noticed a tall, black-haired, Svengalic-looking person in an inner room, and I asked Mr. Cose who he was.

"That is our hypnotizer. The most callous editors succumb to his gaze. Take him with you when you have anything to sell. We rent him at a low figure, consid-ering how useful he is. He has had a busy season, and is tired out, but that is what we pay him for. If he were to die you 'd notice a difference in many of the periodicals. The poorer the material, the better pleased he is to place it. It flatters his vanity."

I assured him that I was something of a hypnotist myself, and, thanking him for his courtesy, was about to come away, when he picked up what looked like a box of tacks and said:

"Here are points for pointless jokes. We don't have much sale for them. Most persons prefer an application of Jokoleine. A recent issue of a comic weekly had sixty jokes and but one point, showing conclusively that points are out of fashion in some editorial rooms.

"A man came in yesterday," rattled on the senior member, "and asked if we bought hand-made jokes, and before we could stop him he said that by hand-made jokes he meant jokes about servant-girls. We gave him the address of 'Punch.'"

At this point I shook hands with Mr. Cose, and as I left he was saying: "For a suitable consideration we will guarantee to call anything a joke that you may bring in, and we will place it without hypnotic aid or the use of Jokoleine. It has been done before."

And as I came away from the sound of his voice, I reflected that it had.

IV

GRIGGS'S MIND

THE other day I met Griggs on the cars. Griggs is the man with the mind. Other people have minds, but they 're not like Griggs's. He lives in Rutherford, New Jersey, and is, like me, a commuter, and as neither of us plays cards nor is interested in politics, and as we have tabooed the weather as a topic, it almost always happens that when we meet, we, or rather he, falls back on his mind as subject for conversation. For my part, my daily newspaper would be all-sufficient for my needs on the way to town; but it pleases Griggs to talk, and it 's bad for my eyes to read on the cars, so I shut them up and cultivate the art of listening, the while Griggs discourses.

I had recently read in the Contributors' Club of the "Atlantic," an article by a woman, who said that the letters of the alphabet seemed to be variously colored in her mind; that is, her mental picture gave to one letter a green hue, to another red, and so on. I spoke of this to Griggs, and he was much interested. He said that the sound of a cornet was always red to him. I asked him whether it made any difference who blew it, but Griggs scorns to notice puns, and he answered: "Not a particle. I don't pretend to explain it, but it is so. Likewise, to me the color of scarlet tastes salt, while crimson is sweet."

I opened my eyes and looked at him in amazement. It sounded like a bit out of "Alice in Wonderland." Then I remembered that it was Griggs who was talking, and that he has a mind. When I don't understand something about Griggs, I lay it to his mind and think no more about it. So I shut my eyes again and listened.

"By the way," said he, "how does time run in your mind?"

"Why, I never thought of its running at all, although it passes quickly enough, for the most part!"

"But has n't it some general direction? Up or down, north or south, east or west?"

"Griggs," said I, "is this your mind?"

"Yes," said he.

"Well, go ahead; fire it off; unfold your kinks!" said I, leaning back in my seat; "but kindly remember that I have no mind, and if you can't put it in words of one syllable, talk slowly so that I can follow you."

He promised to put it as plainly as though he were talking to his youngest, aged three; and, with this assurance, my cerebrum braced itself, so to speak, and awaited the onslaught.

"My idea of the direction of time in all its divisions and subdivisions is as follows—"

"Say, Griggs," said I, "let 's go into the smoker. A little oil of nicotine always makes my brain work easier."

When we were seated in the smoker,

and had each lighted a cigar, he went
on:

"Assuming that I am facing the north,
far in the southwest is the Garden of Eden
and the early years of recorded time.
Moving eastward run the centuries, and
the years to come and the end of the
world are in the far east."

I felt slightly bewizzled, but I gripped
the seat in front of me and said nothing.

"My mental picture of the months of
the year is that January is far to the north.
The months follow in a more or less
zigzag, easterly movement, until we find
that July and August have strayed far
south. But the autumn months zigzag
back, so that by the time December
sweeps coldly by she is twelve months
east of January, and then the new January starts on a road of similar direction.
You still observe that the current of time
sets toward me instead of away from
me."

What could I do but observe that it did?
I had the inside seat, and Griggs has an
insistent way about him, so I generally

2

observe just when he asks me to, and thus avoid friction. Then, too, I always feel flattered when Griggs condescends to talk at me and reveal the wonders of his mind. So I observed heartily, and puffed away at my cigar, while he continued:

"The direction of the week-days is rather hazy in my mind—"

I begged him not to feel low-spirited about it—that it would probably seem clear to him before long; but I don't think he heard me, for he went right on: "But

it is a somewhat undulatory movement
from west to east, Sundays being on the
crest of each wave. Coming to the hours,
I picture them as running, like the famous
mouse, 'down the clock,' the early day-
light being highest. The minutes and
seconds refuse to be marshaled into line,
but go ticking on to eternity helter-skel-
ter, yet none the less inevitably."

I rather admired the independence of
the minutes and seconds in refusing to be
ordered about even by his mind; but, of
course, I did n't tell him so. On the contrary, I congratulated him on the highly
poetic way in which he was voicing his
sentiments.

Just then we came into the station, and
an acquaintance of his buttonholed him
and lugged him off, for Griggs is quite a
favorite, in spite of his mind. I was sorry,
for I had wanted to ask him where the moments and instants seem bound for in his
brain. I did manage, just as we were
leaving the boat at Chambers Street, to
tell him that I was going to be in the
Augustan part of the city at noon, and

would be pleased to take him out to lunch,
if he ran across me; but he must have
mistaken the month, as I ate my luncheon
alone. I dare say he understood me to
say January, and wandered all over Har-
lem looking for me. How unpleasant it
must be to have a mind!

V

THE SIGNALS OF GRIGGS

YOU may remember Griggs as the man who had a mind. At the time that I wrote about that useful member of his make-up he was living out in New Jersey; but he was finally brought to see the error of his ways, and took the top flat in a nine-story house without an elevator, 'way up-town.

The other evening I went to call on the Griggses. He had not yet come home, but his wife let me in and helped me to a sofa to recover from the effects of my climb. I have been up the Matterhorn, Mont Blanc, and Popocatepetl, but I never felt so exhausted as I did after walking up those nine frightful flights. And Mrs. Griggs told me that she thought nothing of running up- and down-stairs a dozen times a day, which was a sad commentary on her truthfulness.

After I was there a few minutes, trying to get used to the notes of two lusty and country-bred children (offspring of Mr. and Mrs. Griggs), there came a feeble and dejected ring at the front-door bell. Mrs. Griggs hastened to the kitchen,—they do not keep a servant (that was their trouble in New Jersey, but now they don't want to),—and after pressing the electric button that opened the front door, she said: "That's poor Mr. Griggs. He must be feeling bad to-night, and I must put the children to bed before he gets up, as he is too nervous to stand their noise."

I was somewhat astonished, but she ripped the clothes off of her buds of promise and popped them into bed with a skill and rapidity that would have secured her a position on the vaudeville stage. After they were covered up she returned to me. Of course Mr. Griggs had not yet arrived, and I asked her how she knew he was tired.

" Why, we have a code of signals.   Mr.
Griggs invented them.   When he has
done well down-town, he taps out a merry

peal on the bell, and then I tell the children to greet him at the hall door and
prepare for a romp.   When the bell rings
sharply I know that he is in no humor for
fun, but will tolerate the children if they

are quiet. But when he rings slowly and faintly, as he did to-night, I always put the dears to bed, as I know he has had bad luck and is worn out."

As she spoke, Griggs opened the hall door and staggered in, weak from his superhuman climb and worn out from his day's work. I said: " Good-by, old man; I 'll call some day when you 're going to give the bell the glad hand. You seem cozily situated." And then I came down in the dumb-waiter, although I suppose it was risky.

What a great thing is an electric bell! But how much greater is an inventive mind like that of Griggs.

VI

À LA SHERLOCK HOLMES

JONES and I recently had occasion to take a drive of four or five miles in upper Connecticut. We were met at the station by Farmer Phelps, who soon had us snugly wrapped in robes and speeding over the frozen highway in a sleigh. It was bitter cold weather—the thermometer reading 3° above zero. We had come up from Philadelphia, and to us such extreme cold was a novelty, which is all we could say for it.

As we rode along, Jones fell to talking about Conan Doyle's detective stories, of which we were both great admirers—the more so as Doyle has declared Philadelphia to be the greatest American city. It turned out that Mr. Phelps was familiar with

the "'Meemoirs' of Sherlock Holmes,"
and he thought there was some "pretty
slick reasonin'" in it. "My girl," said
he, "got the book out er the library an'
read it aout laoud to my woman an' me.
But of course this Doyle had it all cut an'
dried afore he writ it. He worked back-
wards an' kivered up his tracks, an' then
started afresh, an' it seems more wonderful
to the reader than it reely is."

"I don't know," said Jones; "I 've
done a little in the observation line since I
began to read him, and it 's astonishing
how much a man can learn from inanimate
objects, if he uses his eyes and his brain
to good purpose. I rarely make a mistake."

Just then we drove past an outbuilding.
The door of it was shut. In front of it,
in a straight row and equidistant from
each other, lay seven cakes of ice, thawed
out of a water-pan.

"There," said Jones; "what do we gather
from those seven cakes of ice and that
closed door?"

I gave it up.

Mr. Phelps said nothing.

Jones waited impressively a moment, and then said quite glibly: "The man who lives there keeps a flock of twelve hens—not Leghorns, but probably Plymouth Rocks or some Asiatic variety. He attends to them himself, and has good success with them, although this is the seventh day of extremely cold weather."

I gazed at him in admiration.

Mr. Phelps said nothing.

"How do you make it all out, Jones?" said I.

"Well, those cakes of ice were evidently formed in a hens' drinking-pan. They are solid. The water froze a little all day long, and froze solid in the night. It was thawed out in the morning and left lying there, and the pan was refilled. There are seven cakes of ice; therefore there has been a week of very cold weather. They are side by side: from this we gather that it was a methodical man who attended to them; evidently no hireling, but the goodman himself. Methodical in little things, methodical in greater ones; and method spells success with hens. The thickness of the ice also proves that comparatively little water was drunk; consequently he keeps a small flock. Twelve is the model number among advanced poultrymen, and

he is evidently one. Then, the clearness of the ice shows that the hens are not excitable Leghorns, but fowl of a more sluggish kind, although whether Plymouth Rocks or Brahmas or Langshans, I can't say. Leghorns are so wild that they are apt to stampede through the water and roil it. The closed door shows he has the good sense to keep them shut up in cold weather.

" To sum up, then, this wide-awake poultryman has had wonderful success, in spite of a week of exceptionally cold weather, from his flock of a dozen hens of some large breed. How 's that, Mr. Phelps? Is n't it almost equal to Doyle? "

" Yes; but not accordin' to Hoyle, ez

ye might say," said he.   "Your reasonin'
is good, but it ain't quite borne aout by
the fac's.   In the fust place, this is the fust
reel cold day we 've. hed this winter.
Secon'ly, they ain't no boss to the place,
fer she 's a woman.   Thirdly, my haouse
is the nex' one to this, an' my boy an'
hers hez be'n makin' those ice-cakes fer
fun in some old cream-pans.   Don't take
long to freeze solid in this weather.   An',
las'ly, it ain't a hen-haouse, but an ice-
haouse."

The sun rode with unusual quietness
through the heavens.   We heard no song
of bird.   The winds were whist.   All nature was silent.

So was Jones.

VII

MY SPANISH PARROT

HAVE two maiden aunts living down in Maine, on the edge of the woods. Their father was a deaf-and-dumb woodsman, and their mother died when they were small, and they hardly see a soul from one year's end to the other. The consequence is, they 're the simplest, dearest old creatures one ever saw. They don't know what evil means. They pass their days knitting and working in their garden. The quarterly visits of the itinerant preacher who deals out the gospel in that region, and my occasional trips up there, constitute the only chances they have of mingling with the outside world, and they 're as happy and unsophisticated as birds.

30

A year ago I took up a parrot that I 'd
bought of a sailor. The bird had a cold
when I got it, and was n't saying a word;
but the sailor vouched for its character,
and I thought it would be a novelty and
company for the old ladies, so I took it
along. They 'd never seen a parrot before, and they could n't thank me enough.
I told them that when it got over its cold
it would talk; and then it occurred to me
that as the sailor of which I bought it was
a Spaniard, the bird would be likely to
speak that tongue. "So you 'll be able
to learn Spanish," said I; and they were
mightily pleased at the notion.

In about two months I received a letter
from Aunt Linda, saying that the bird
was the greatest company in the world,
and they did n't know what they 'd do
without him. "And," wrote my aunt,
"the bird is a great talker of Spanish, and
we have learned much of that strange
tongue."

I was amused at the idea of those
maiden aunts of mine talking Spanish, and
the next week, being in the vicinity, I

took the stage over to where they live, about fifteen miles from any railroad.

They saw me alight, and came out to meet me—two pretty, sweet, prim-looking old ladies. I kissed them both heartily, and then Aunt Linda said, in her gentle voice: " I 'm so glad you 've come, you dear old blankety-blank blank blank boy. That 's Spanish."

I nearly fell off my perch, but I managed to keep a straight face, and then dear Aunt Jane said softly and proudly: " Why the blankety-blank blank don't you come to see us oftener, you blankety-blank blank boy? "

It made my blood run cold to hear the oaths those innocent creatures poured out on me all day. The parrot followed me around, and perked his. head on one side, as much as to say, " Are n't they apt pupils? " but he never opened his mouth to talk—and there really was n't any need. They kept me supplied with conversation on their quiet doings, all interlarded with their new-found " Spanish," until it was time to go to bed.

I had n't the heart to tell them that the tongue in which they were so fluent was not Spanish; and as their hearts were as pure as a baby's, and they saw no one, I said nothing; but when I left, early next morning, I was careful to bid them good-

by out of ear-shot of the stage-coach, and it 's lucky I did, for the torrent of billings- gate that they poured fondly over me would have caused the occupants of the coach to think entirely unwarranted things of the old ladies.

As I climbed up to the seat by the driver,

3

a man got out of the stage and walked up to the house.

"Good heavens! who's that?" I asked of the driver.

"Thet," said he, "is the Methody preacher makin' his quarterly visit to th' old ladies."

VIII

"TO MEET MR. CAVENDISH"

THE card read, "To meet Mr. Cavendish." I had not been in Boston long, and I must confess to a poor head for names, so I had no idea who Mr. Cavendish was or what he had done, but as he was to be at Mrs. Emerson's, I knew he had done something.

There were only five guests there, besides Mr. Cavendish, when I arrived, and after we were introduced it so happened that Cavendish and I found ourselves talking together.

He looked tired, so I said as a starter: "Don't you find your work exhausting?" I thought I'd play "twenty questions" with him, and determine what he had done.

"Sometimes it is, very. The expenditure of force fairly makes my throat ache."

It was easy. He was probably a Wagnerian singer.

"I suppose you have to be very careful about your throat."

"Why, no," he said; "I never think about my throat."

He was n't a singer.

"Well, you 're in love with your art."

He smiled. "Yes, I 'm in love with it."

I was in despair. What was he?

But now I would nail him. "What are your methods of work, Mr. Cavendish?"

"Oh, I don't spend much time in over-elaboration. My brush-strokes are very broad."

Ah, a painter! "Exactly," I said. "You like a free hand."

He said: "After all, the words are everything."

Ah, a writer! "Yes," said I; "your words are everything to the public."

"I hope so. I try to make them so," he said modestly.

Now I felt easier, and proceeded to praise him specifically.

"Which do you like best—to make your public laugh or cry? or do you aim to instruct it?"

"It is easy to make persons laugh, so I suppose I like rather to bring them to tears. As for instruction, there are those who say it is not our province to instruct."

"But you do all three, Mr. Cavendish."

He bowed as if he thought I had hit it.

I said: "To those who are familiar with your work there is something that makes you just the man to pick up for a quarter of an hour."

His blank expression showed that I had made some mistake. He is a tall, portly man, and he seemed alarmed at the prospect of being picked up. A fall would be serious.

"I don't quite get your meaning, but I suppose you refer to the men about town who stray in for a few minutes."

It seemed a queer way to express it,

3*

but I replied: "Oh, yes; just to browse. You repay browsing, Mr. Cavendish."

He smiled reminiscently. "Speaking of browsing, when I was told to go ahead

on Richelieu, I browsed a long time in the British Museum getting up data."

What, a painter, after all? I forgot all else he had said, and told him I thought he was as happy as Sargent or Whistler.

"Yes; I don't let little things worry me

much. Sometimes the paint gives out at a critical time in a small town."

Good heaven! Why should the paint give out in a small town at a critical time? *Was* he a painter, after all? Could he be a traveling sign-painter?

"Does it bother you to work up in the air?"

"That 's an original way of putting it," said he, with a genial laugh. "To play to the grand stand, as it were. Oh, no; a man must do more or less of that to succeed."

I was shocked. "You surely don't believe in desecrating nature! Sermons in stones, if you will, but not sermons *on* stones. You would n't letter the Palisades if you had a chance, would you?"

He edged away from me, and said: "Oh, no, I would n't letter the Palisades, although I dare say my man of affairs would be glad to."

Then I gave up. His man of affairs! He must be a gentleman of leisure to have a man of affairs.

And then up came Ticknor Fields, the

dramatic critic, and said: "How do you do, Mr. Cavendish? Let me congratulate you upon your success as Richelieu. At last a successor to Booth has been found."

I went and drank a glass of iced water. My throat was dry.

IX

INSTINCT SUPPLIED TO HENS

COMPANY has just been formed in New Jersey for the purpose of supplying instinct to hens. Such well-known farmers as Frank R. Stockton, Russell Sage, and Bishop Potter are stock-holders in it, and if filling a long-felt want is all that is needed, the success of the company is already assured.

No one who has ever dabbled in hens needs to be told that the gallinaceous birds have no instinct whatever. Some have blind luck, but a hen with instincts in good working order would be an anomaly.

I visited Mr. Stockton at his extensive farm in New Jersey in order to find out what I could about the project. I found him in a frock-coat and overalls, training a squash-vine up a maple-tree. He greeted me cordially, and asked me to come and see his tomato-trenches. He also showed me quite an extensive area covered with birch poles for his radishes to climb on. He was very urbane, and willingly told me all about the company.

"No man," said he, sitting down on one of his largest cucumbers and motioning me to a seat on another, "who has ever kept hens but has wondered why they were not provided with a good common-sense brand of instinct. No animal needs instinct more than a hen. It was to supply this need that our company was formed. You know that if you put a hen on cobblestones, she will brood over them with all the devotion possible, and if at the end of three weeks you put a baby chicken under her, her—what you might term false instinct—will cause her to cluck and call to the cobble to come forth and follow her."

I admitted the force of his remark, because when a boy I had once set a hen on

some green apples, and she had covered
them without a murmur for a week, when
I took pity on her and replaced them with

real eggs.   The following day, not liking
the feeling of the eggs, she left them, and
gathering together the apples that I had
left scattered upon the barn floor, she sat
on them again.

I told this experience to Mr. Stockton,
and he said: " If she 'd had a few of our
instinct-powders before sitting she would
have repudiated the fraud at once.   Is it
instinct, or the lack of it," he continued,
" that makes a heavy Light Brahma plant
a ponderous and feathered foot upon her
offspring and listen calmly to their expir-
ing peeps?   It 's lack of it; she needs one
of our powders."

I made a mental calculation of the
number of chickens that I had seen sacri-

ficed in that way by motherly and good-
natured hens who would have felt hurt if
you had told them that they did not know
how to bring up their young.

We had risen, and were now walking as
we talked, and we soon came to Mr. Stockton's corn-trellises. He is a great believer
in climbing, and it was a pretty sight to
see his corn waving in the breeze that blew
through the trellis netting.

" Poultry-raising would be an unmixed
joy," said he, as he picked a turnip and
offered it to me, " if a fellow was n't con-
stantly running up against this lack of instinct on the part of the fowls. If a hen
had instinct she 'd know enough to keep
her mouth shut when she laid an egg; but
as it is, she cackles away like a woman
with a secret, and before she knows it her
egg is on the way to the table. But the
aim of our company will be to furnish each
hen with a sufficient amount of instinct
to render her profitable to her master.
When she has that instinct she will not sit
on her nest long after her eggs have been
removed; she will not walk off through the

long grass, calling to her brood to follow
her, when the chicks have all been swal-
lowed by the treacherous domestic cat;
and she will not do the thousand and
one things that any hen, no matter what
her breed or breeding, will do, as it is."

I told Mr. Stockton, as I shook hands
with him in parting, that there was not a
farmer, either amateur or professional, in
the whole Union, who would not be glad
to purchase a package of his instinct-
powders; and as I left the genial granger,
he was putting cushions under his water-
melons so that they would not get bruised
by contact with the earth.

X

A SPRING IDYL

IT was a bright morning in early spring — one of the delightful, languorous days that take the sap out of one and make the life of the tramp seem blissful. The maples were just putting forth their delicate crimson leaves, and a warm south wind bore into the city the smell of fresh earth. Ah, what longings were stirred up in the breast of Key, Pattit & Company's office-boy, country-bred, but pent up in the city for a twelve-month past! Oh, for one day in the country! He would follow the winding trout-stream from its source in ·Perkins's meadow until it emptied into the Naugatuck, and with angleworms dug from the famous spot north of the barn he would

lure the coy trout from their shaded lurk-
ing-places.

Hark! what was that? The "drowsy
tinkling" of a cow-bell—of cow-bells.
What sweet music!
It drove him wild
with longing, as
louder and ever
louder, and nearer
and yet nearer,
came the sound of
bells. Ah, he could
see Jerry, the hired
man, driving the
cows up the grassy
lane. As usual, Bet-
ty, the Jersey, was
in the lead. And
there was greedy

Daisy, lingering to crop the rich grass that
grew along the lane until Jerry's "Whe-e-y,
whe-e-y!" should bid her hurry on. And
there were the twin heifers, Nanny and
Fanny, perfectly matched Holsteins. And
in the rear, plodding on with dignity and
fatness, was Diana, the great Devon.

How the bells jangled! Surely it was
not seeming, but actuality. They were
right outside on the street.

Impulsively he ran to the office window
and looked down with boyish anticipation.

" Jingle-jangle!"   went   the   bells.
" Rha-ags, rha-ags, any ol' rha-ags! "
shouted the ragman.

XI

AN INVERTED SPRING IDYL

IT was a bright morning in the early spring, a time to call forth poetic fancies in the mind of the most prosaic; and Jack was more imaginative than many boys. He had been spending. the winter at his uncle's in the country, and these warm, languorous days had made him long for New York once more. He sat astride of a maple-branch, on which the crimson leaves were just peeping out. Ah me, what would he not give to be back in the city! He leaned back against the tree-trunk and gave himself over to day-dreams.

The boys on his block were spinning tops. Oh, for a good hard city pavement for just five minutes, that he might do the same. Through the hazy air came the anything but drowsy tinklings of the grip-men's gongs; a scissors-grinder blew his horn; and the exciting clang of an ambu-lance-gong split the air as the ambu-lance rattled over the Belgian blocks. Oh, for an hour of the dear city in the happy springtime!   To hear once more the piano-organ and the harp, and the thousand de-lightful sounds that were so lamentably absent from the country!

What was that? Did he hear bells? Yes, surely it was the ragman. He had

never realized how he loved him.   He could see the fellow, lean and ragged and bent, pushing his cart, while from his lips came the cry of " Rha-ags! rha-ags! " and from the sagging cord the sweet bells jingled. Yes, sure-ly it was the bells.

All thought of the lonely country faded away, and he was once more home; the boys were just around the corner, and the bells were coming nearer.

Their tintinnabulations grew so loud that he waked from his day-dream and saw—not a familiar and beloved city sight, but a tiresome herd of cows coming home to be milked, their harsh bells jangling out of tune.

XII

AT THE CHESTNUTS' DINNER

THE Hoary Chestnuts were assembling for their annual Christmas dinner. Sweet music was discoursed by the chestnut bell, and, despite their age and many infirmities, the members wore a look of gaiety suitable to so festive an occasion. There was not a young joke among them, excepting a very few special jokes like the Trolley variety and the Cuban War joke, and these, from overwork, were as superannuated-looking as the oldest there. Not a well-known joke but would come. Of course they would all live until the next dinner, for an old joke is immortal; but this yearly gathering was their only chance to meet and shake hands generally, as during the rest

of the year they would be scattered
through the columns of the dailies and the
comic weeklies, and their meetings would
be chance ones.

The hearty old Mother-in-law joke
chatted gaily with that venerable old lady,
I-will-be-a-sister-to-you. The adorable
twins, Ballet-girl's-age and Ballet-girl's-
scant-raiment, were the center of a group
made up of the haughty Rich-plumber, the
Rejected-manuscript, the Slow-messenger-
boy, the Sleeping-watchman, and a good
score of Boarding-house jokes. The one
called Boarding-house-coffee felt a little
stirred up at the false report that he was
losing ground, and he had an unsettled
look upon his swarthy and senile features.
The idea was absurd on the face of it, for
undoubtedly he would be printed in every
section of the country before the month
was out, as he had been any month for
decades past. The Summer jokes, including, of course, the star jest, the Summer-
girl, looked comparatively fresh, as they
were not in use the year round, like Her-
father's-foot, for instance, or that other

4*

member of the same family, the Chicago-
girl's-foot, that year in and year out is
used as a laugh-producer.

The Boston jokes, icy and reserved, sat
apart from the rest, and glared at each

other in a near-sighted way. The Freak
jokes, on the contrary, were hail-fellow-
well-met with every one, and their vulgar
laughter could be heard everywhere.

A good deal of sympathy was expressed
for Actor-walking-home, for he was so
feeble that he had to be helped across the

room by Weary Wraggles. The Tramps were out in force. Tickets to the dinner were five dollars, and it was rumored that Dusty Rhodes had worked his way in, but upon reflection the idea will be seen to be preposterous.

There was a strong smell of cloves in the air when the door opened for the entrance of old Between-the-acts. He came arm in arm with that other favorite, Detained-at-the-lodge.

The Farmer jokes came in a little late. Their chores had detained them. But their entrance was hailed with delight by a body of paragraphers who sat in the gallery as representatives of the press, and who had paid many a bill, thanks to the Farmers.

A joke, rather square-cut and with wheels in his head, came in with a " Where is she ? " look on his dial, and as soon as he said, " I expected to meter here," he was recognized as Big-gas-bill. The Wheel jokes were conspicuous by their absence. This was explained on the ground that they were not yet old enough to become Hoary Chestnuts, and, as a relentless paragrapher remarked, "They were tired, anyhow."

The last ones to arrive were the Cannibal and Tough-missionary; and the chairman of the reception committee having assigned them seats at opposite ends of the table, all sat down, and the annual balloting to determine what had been the most popular joke of the year was begun.

Many voted for themselves, notably the Boston-bean joke and the Rich-plumber; but when the votes were counted, the successful person proved to be neither of these, but a hideously homely woman with a perpetual smirk upon her face.

"Who's she?" asked one paragrapher of another.

"You don't know her? Why, that's My-face-is-my-fortune-then-you-must-be-dead-broke."

And they crowned her with laurel as unquestionably the most perennially popular joke.

XIII

THE ROUGH WORDS SOCIETY

HE other day I passed a house on which there was a sign that read, "The Rough Words Society." Curious to know what it could mean, I retraced my steps, and met a millionaire whom I had long admired from a distance —he was so rich—just leaving the door. It was a presumptuous thing to do, but I said, "How do you do, sir?" in my best manner. He bowed with some urbanity, and I ventured to ask him whether he could tell me anything about the society whose rooms he had just left. "I thought maybe you were president, sir, or one of the directors."

"No; I am a subscriber. If you care

to hear about it, come down-town with me, as I am in a hurry," he replied.

A minute later I was actually in a cab with a millionaire! My heart beat hard, but I kept my ears open, and he said:

"You see, a multi-millionaire like myself seldom meets the frank side of people. They are afraid of offending me," he observed, as we went on our way. "My pastor hangs on my words, my clerks speak in subdued tones, my servants hardly dare address me; and yet, I was once a barefoot boy, and was considered a scapegrace by the village people who to-day bow ceremoniously when I chance to go back to my native place. Well, such sycophancy becomes wearing, and I often used to wish that some one would tell me I lied, or some other wholesome truth."

I shook my head deprecatingly, whereat he seemed annoyed, but went on: "One day I was passing through the street where you met me, and I saw the sign, and, like yours, my curiosity was excited, and I went in. I found a room somewhat like a telegraph-office in appearance. A very

downright, uncompromising-looking man
sat at a roll-top desk, while ranged against
the wall were several men of exceedingly
bluff appearance. 'Can you tell me what
the aims of your society are?' I asked the
man. 'Certainly I can,' said he. 'I
would n't be here if I could n't.' Not a
cringe, you see. It was refreshing.
'Well, will you?' 'It depends,' he said.
'What do you want to know for? Are
you a reporter, or do you want to subscribe?'

"I suddenly divined the purpose of the
society, and I said: 'I want to subscribe.
What are your terms?' 'A hundred dollars for a fifteen-minute séance, one hundred and fifty dollars for a half-hour, and
two hundred dollars for a full hour.' I
handed him a hundred-dollar bill and
said: 'Explain.' 'Jack,' said he, address-
ing a bullet-headed man who was sitting
with his feet up on the railing that divided
the room into two parts, 'give this man a
piece of your mind.' Jack ran through a
directory of millionaires containing photo-
graphs and short biographical sketches,

and when he had found mine he sailed in
and talked as plainly as any one could.
Did n't say a word that was n't true; but
he did n't mince his language, and he was
no more abashed by my position in the
world than if I 'd still been a barefoot boy.
It did me good.   He overhauled many of
my acts during the last twenty years, and
talked to me like a Dutch uncle.   Re-
freshed?   Why, a Turkish bath is not in it
for comfort!   After he 'd finished, the
manager said I could have an extra in the

way of a little billingsgate if I cared to;
but, if I was born poor, I have always had
gentlemanly instincts, and so I told him I
guessed not.

"As I came away, he said: 'Glad to
have you call any time that you feel the
need of a few plain truths. We have a
minister who says what he thinks in a very
trenchant way, and I 'm sure you 'd be
glad to let him give you a raking over.
Here 's one of our cards. Drop in any
time you 're passing. If, for any reason,
you are not able to come, we can send a
man to take up his abode in your house,
or to give you half-hour talks from the
shoulder, and you can have a monthly account with us. Say a good word for us
to any of your plutocratic friends who are
tired of sycophancy. Good day, old
man.'"

I was aghast at what he had told me,
and I said: "I wonder at his temerity!"

"Why," said the millionaire, "I love
him for it! After a directors' meeting,
when I have been kotowed to until my
gorge rises, I just drop in there, and they

tell me unpleasant truths about myself with the utmost freedom,—you see, they keep posted about me,—and I come out feeling a hundred per cent. better. Well, here 's my office. Good day, young man."

" Good day, sir, and thank you for letting me ride with you."

He slammed the door as if vexed, and as he approached the door of his office a negro ran to open it, and two office-boys took his coat and hat, and I envied the great man from the bottom of my heart.

XIV

A NEW USE FOR HORSES

MET Scott Bindley the other day. Scott is a great schemer. I think he must be related on his mother's side to Colonel Sellers. At any rate, there is n't a day in the year that he does n't think of some idea that should interest capital, although capital, somehow, fails to become interested. As soon as he saw me he said:

"Got a great scheme. Small fortune in it for the right parties."

"What is it?" I asked.

"Come into some cheap lunch-place, and I 'll blow myself off to a meal and give you the particulars."

So it came to pass that we were soon

seated in a restaurant which, if cheap, is clean—a combination rarer than need be.

"You 've probably noticed that the more automobiles there are in use, the more breakdowns there are."

I could but admit that it was so.

"Well, what is more useless than a broken-down motor-wagon?"

I would have suggested "Two," but Bindley hates warmed-up jokes, so I refrained and told him that I gave it up.

"It is n't a conundrum," said he, irritably. "Nothing in the world is more useless than a broken-down motor. There are some vehicles of a box-like pattern that can be used as hen-houses when they have outlived their initial usefulness, but who wants a hen-house on Fifth Avenue, corner of Twenty-fifth Street, or any other place where a motor vehicle gives out? The more I thought this over, the more I felt that something was needed to make a disabled automobile of some use, and I saw that the man who would supply that something could make money hand over fist. So I devoted a great deal of time

to the subject, and at last I hit it.
Horses."

" Horses what? " said I.

" Why, horses to supply the motive
power.   Horses are getting to be a drug

in the market, and can be bought dirt-
cheap.   That being the case, I am going
to interest capitalists in the scheme, and
then we will buy up a lot of horses and
distribute them at different points in the
city.   Then, when a man is out in his
automobile and breaks down, he will tele-
phone to the nearest station and get a
horse.   This can easily be hitched to the
motor by a contrivance that I intend to
patent, and then the horse can drag the
wagon to the nearest power-house, where
it can be restocked with electricity, or gas,
or naphtha, or whatever is wanted.   Is n't

it a great scheme? Why, sir, I can see in the future the plan enlarged so that people will always take a horse along with them when they go a-motoring, and, if anything happens, there they are with the good old horse handy. Talk about the horseless age! Why, horses are just entering upon a new sphere of usefulness."

I opened my mouth to speak, but he went on: " I tell you that if I can get the holders of automobile stock to coöperate with me I 'll stop eating at places like this."

A look of such sweet content overspread his features that I told him to put me down for ten shares as soon as his company was organized. That was a month ago, and I have n't gotten my stock yet. But motors are becoming stalled every day.

XV

A CALCULATING BORE

Y friend Bings is one of those habitual calculators—one of the kind that says if all the teeth that have been extracted since the first dentist began business were to be used for paving purposes in Hades, the good-resolutions contractor would be out of a job for ten thousand years. He thinks in numbers, and if he were a minister he would get all his texts from the same source.

The other day he saw me first on a ferry-boat, and immediately buttonholed me. Said he: "How sad it is to think that so much labor goes for naught!"

I knew that I was in for one of his calculations; but I also knew that it would be useless to try to head him off.

He stroked his beard, and said, with an imitation of thoughtfulness:

" Every day in this Empire State one million human beings go to bed tired be-

cause you and I and the rest leave butter on our plates and don't eat our crusts."

I told him that I was astonished, but that he would have to elucidate.

" The farmers sow 8,000,000 bushels of useless grain,—grain that eventually goes out to sea on the refuse-scows,—they milk 50,000 cows to no other purpose than to produce sour or spilled milk, they allow their valuable hens to lay 1,654,800,001 eggs that will serve no better purpose than to spatter some would-be Booth or lie neglected in some out-of-the-way corner, while their wives are making 1,008,983 pounds of butter that will be left on the edges of plates and thrown into the refuse-pail. If they did n't sow the useless grain, or fuss over the hens that lay the un-used eggs, or draw the milk that is destined to sour, or make the butter that is to orna-ment the edges of the china disks, they would be able to go to bed merely health-ily tired instead of overworked, and fewer farmers would commit suicide, and fewer farmers' wives would go insane."

His eyes gleamed, and I knew that, as he would put it, his pulse was going so fast that if it were revolutions of a locomotive-wheel it would take only so long to go somewhere.

"And what is your remedy for all this?" asked I, with becoming, if mock, interest.

"Let us help ourselves to no more than we want at table, buy our eggs a week earlier, drink our milk the day before, eat our bread before it is too dry, and in six months' time there will be a reduced State death-rate, more vacancies in the insane asylums, 1,456,608 rosy cheeks where to-day there are that many pale ones—"

5*

Just then the ferry-boat's gates were lifted, and as we went our several ways, in the hurry that is characteristic of 7,098,111 Americans out of eight millions, I thought that, if all the brains of all the arithmetical cranks were used in place of wood-pulp to make into paper, we writers would get our pads for nothing.

XVI

AN URBAN GAME

 GAME that is much played in hot weather by persons who are addicted to the department-store habit is called " Where can I find it?" It is played by means of counters, and its duration is often a whole morning in length. To the looker-on it is much like golf, it seems so aimless; and it is aimless, but it has the advantages over golf that it can be played in the city and does not necessitate the services of a caddy. Over a score take a hand in it from first to last, but only one is " it," and she or he displays the only activity necessary to the game. Only those who are of tough build should undertake to play it on a hot day, as it is extremely debilitating.

To make the game long and interesting, you should enter the store and ask for something a little unusual that you may have seen advertised somewhere. For instance, you go to the glove counter and ask for a preparation for making soup, called " Soupina." I am not advertising anything, as the name is fictitious, but it will serve to illustrate my meaning. The particular embodiment of haughtiness at the glove counter will think that you mean some kind of soap, and will frigidly direct you to the perfumery department, " pillar No. 8." You go there simply because it is your move, and you repeat your inquiry, adding that you think it 's put up in bottles.

" Bottled goods," is the quick rejoinder, " fourth floor."

The elevator bears you to the grocery department, and you ask for " bottled goods."

" Pillar 20."

At pillar No. 20 you are made to realize what a poor worm you are, and you turn to pillar 10, as requested, that being the canned-goods department. That clerk will undoubtedly misunderstand your order and will direct you to the basement, "pillar 15." You hurry down in the elevator, and come face to face with the mouse-trap counter. How you go from ladies' underwear to carpets, to furniture, to the telegraph-office, to the dental parlors, to the menagerie, to the restaurant, to the lace goods, to every department known to a modern city under one roof, you can best find out for yourself, but of one thing you may be sure—you will never find "Soupina."

At last, dazed and heated and leg-weary, you find yourself in the oath-registering room. This is a little room that is in every well-equipped department-store, and fills a long-felt want, for all shoppers, at one time or another, wish to register an oath. Whether you register or not, the game is now over, and you have lost; there is no possibility of winning. And yet, so fascinating is the sport that as soon as you have recovered the use of your muscles you will be eager to play again.

XVII

"DE GUSTIBUS"

I T was on one of the cannibal isl-
ands, and a family of cannibals
were discussing the pleasures of
the table on their front piazza while they
waited for dinner to be announced.   Their
eldest daughter, a slim, acidulous-looking
girl, just home from boarding-school, and
full of fads and " isms," had said that, for
her part, she did not care for human flesh
at all, and was of the opinion that pigs or
lambs, or even cows, would make just as
good eating as the tenderest enemy ever
captured or the juiciest missionary ever
broiled.

" How disgusting! " said her brother,
a lusty young cannibal who had once eaten
two Salvation Army lassies at a sitting.

" Really, if you get such unpleasant notions at school, it would be better for you to stay at home. My gorge rises at the idea. Ugh! "

" Papa," said dear little kinky-haired E. Taman, the peacemaker of the family, changing the subject, " why are missionaries better eating than our neighbors and enemies? "

" Probably because they are apt to be cereal-eaters," said her father, the cannibal chief; " although one of the most delicious missionaries I ever tasted was a Boston lady who had been raised on beans. She was a Unitarian. Your Unitarians generally make good eating. There 's a good deal of the milk of human kindness in them, and that makes them excellent roasters. Now, you take a hard-shell Baptist, and you might as well eat a ' shore dinner ' at once. They need a heap of steaming, and they 're apt to be watery when all 's said and done. But it must be confessed they have more taste than a wishy-washy agnostic."

" I think the most unsatisfactory of the

lot," said his wife, "is your Presbyterian. He's pretty sure to be dry and gnarly, and good for nothing but fricasseeing. But I think that for all-round use, although they have n't the delicacy of the Unitarian, the Methodist is what you might call the Plymouth Rock of missionaries. He's generally fat, and he has n't danced himself dry, and he's good for a pot-roast or any old thing. By the way, we 're go-ing to have one to-day. I must go and tell the cook to baste him well."

The old grandfather, who had hitherto taken no part in the conversation, said at this point: "Well, as you know, in my day I have been something of an epicure, and I have tasted every variety of dish known to cannibals. I don't care for fresh-killed meat, no matter of what denomination it is, and while I don't wish to

be considered a sectarian, yet I do think
that if you want a dish that is capable of
a good deal of trimming and fancy fixings'
get hold of an Episcopal missionary; and,
to me, the chief beauty of the Episcopalian
is that he 's apt to be a little high."

XVIII

"BUFFUM'S BUSTLESS BUFFERS"

I WAS looking at a rather startling picture in the morning paper of a man who had fallen from a seventh-story window and had been instantly killed. The man in the seat next to me—we were on the elevated—said: "I 'll do away with all those accidents soon."

I turned and looked at him. He was a lean-faced, hollow-eyed man, full of nervous starts, and quick of speech.

"What do you mean?" asked I, somewhat puzzled.

"Oh, nothing; oh, nothing at all," he replied, as if sorry he had spoken. "I do not wish to be laughed at. I am no Keely motor man to be laughed at. I spoke without thought."

I fancied there was a story in him, and so I drew him out, and he said in short, quick sentences, but in so low a tone that I had to strain my ears to hear him:

" I am Burgess Buffum, the inventor of Buffum's Bustless Buffers."

He paused with rhetorical effect, and nodded and blinked his eyes; and I, duly impressed, asked him what the buffers were supposed to buff.

" Children at open windows. Painters on scaffolds. Panic-stricken flyers from fires. Mountain-climbers. In fact, all persons whose business or duty or pleasure carries them to unsafe heights. My buffers are filled with air, and you can't bust 'em. Child can fill 'em. Foot-pump, puff, puff, puff, and there you are. They are made of rubber and weigh next to nothing. Painter at work on scaffold; hears rope breaking; seizes one of my patent buffers; holds it carelessly in his right hand until within five feet of the pavement; then catches it with both

hands, holds it in front of him as a shield, and falls with it under him. Merely pleasant titillation. Up at once; mends rope; resumes painting; undertaker foiled; no funeral; money saved; put in bank, or invested in stock in my company—"

"But," said I, interrupting him, "suppose the buffer is n't handy?"

"Ah, that 's his lookout. It must be handy. No business to take chances when safeguard is on scaffolding with him. Or child playing on fire-escape; careful mother puts two of my buffers out there;

warns child not to fall without one; goes about her work care-free; child feels that it is about to fall; clutches buffer; goes down like painter; pleasant ride; child enjoys it; perfect confidence in my buffer; holds it under him; arrives seated; no deleterious effect; continues play in street. Object-lesson in favor of my invention. Child takes orders for my buffers; gets commission from me. Sells dozens—"

Just then the guard called out, " Forty-second Street! " and a man whom I had not noticed before, but who wore an air of authority, and who sat next to Buffum, rose and, touching him on the arm, said, " Come."

And before I could get the inventor's address he had left the train.

But I fancy that

BURGESS BUFFUM, ESQ.,
Bloomingdale,

will reach him.

AT THE LITERARY COUNTER

XIX

"THE FATHER OF SANTA CLAUS"

THE Successful Author dropped in at the club and looked around for some one to whom he might talk shop. He spied the Timid Aspirant in the corner, and asked him to sit down. The Timid Aspirant blushed all over, and felt that better days were dawning for him, because the Successful Author's name was in every one's mouth.

" Have much trouble to sell your stuff, my boy ? "

" Oh, I suppose I ought n't to complain."

" Never destroy a manuscript, my boy. You don't, do you ? "

"Sometimes, sir."

"Ah, don't. You never know when it will become valuable. Anything written has its niche somewhere."

Then the Successful Author sank back in his arm-chair and continued reminiscently: "I'll never forget how one of my articles fared. It was the fourth or fifth thing that I had written, and it was called 'The Father of Santa Claus.' I liked it better than any editor has ever liked anything of mine."

The Timid Aspirant nodded sympathetically, and the Successful Author continued: "I sent it to the 'Prospect,' and it came back promptly. Did I destroy it? Not at all. I pigeonholed it, and next year I sent it to them again. Again it came back, and once more I laid it to rest for a twelvemonth, and then bombarded the 'Prospect' with it. This sort of thing went on for several years, until at last, to save time, the editor had a special form of rejection printed for it that ran about as follows:

"DEAR SIR: The time of year has come once more when we reject your story, 'The Father of Santa Claus.' It would not seem like the sweet Christmas season if we did not have a chance to turn it down.   Yours respectfully,
        "EDITOR THE PROSPECT."

"Let you down easy each year, did n't he?"

"Yes.   Well, in course of time my price went up. At the start I 'd have been tickled to death to get five dollars for the thing, but now I knew that if the editor ever did change his mind I 'd get at least fifty, so I kept at it.   Well, it was last year that my collection of stories made such a hit, and since then I 've been so busy filling orders for short stories that I forgot to send my dear old mossback out this year. But day before yesterday I received a note from the editor of the 'Prospect' asking for a Christmas sketch.   Now was my opportunity.   I wrote back:

"Sorry I have n't anything new, but it struck me that you might like to look at an old thing of

mine called ' The Father of Santa Claus,' and if
you care to consider its publication I 'll let it go
for a couple of hundred, just for the sake of old
times.

I inclosed the story, and just before
coming here I received a check for two
hundred dollars."

"What moral do you deduce
from this, sir?"

"Don't ever sell anything
until you 've gotten a big
reputation."

"Do you mind talk-
ing a little more
shop?" asked the
Timid Aspirant.
Somehow he lost
his timidity when
talking to his re-
nowned friend.

"Of course not. No one really does,
though some affect to. Most talk is shop
talk. It may relate to plumbing, or to
dry-goods, or to painting, or to babies,
but it is of the shop shoppy, as a rule,
only ' literary shop talk,' as Ford calls it,

is more interesting to an outsider than the other kinds. What particular department of our shop did you want me to handle?"

" I wanted to ask you if you believed in cutting a man's work—in other words, do you believe in blue-penciling?"

" Ah, my boy, I see that they have been coloring your manuscript with the hateful crayon. No, I don't believe in it. I dislike it now because it mars my work, and I used to hate it because it took money from my purse. Let me tell you a little incident.

" One time, years ago, I wrote an article, and after it was done I figured on what I would get for it and with it. If I sold it to a certain monthly I had in mind I should receive enough to buy a new hat, a new suit, a pair of shoes, ditto of socks, and a necktie, for all of which I stood in sore need. I hied me forth in all the exuberance of youth and bore my manuscript to the editor. As he was feeling pretty good, he said he 'd read it while I waited. At last he laid it down and said :

'That's a pretty good story.' My heart leaped like an athlete. 'But'—my heart stopped leaping and listened—'it will need a little cutting, and I'll do it now, if you wish.'"

"Poor fellow!" said the Timid Aspirant, sympathetically.

"Well, the first thing that editor did was to cut the socks off of it; then he made a deep incision in the hat; then he slashed away at the trousers and did some scattered cutting, and at last handed the manuscript to me that I might see the havoc he had wrought in my prospective wardrobe. Dear man, I had a vest and a necktie left, and that was all. And it would have been the same if it had been a dinner."

The Timid Aspirant shuddered.

"Many a young author has seen the soup and the vegetables, and at last the steak, fade away under the terrible obliterating power of the indigo crayon, and lucky is he if a sandwich and a glass of water remain after the editor's fell work. Blessed is that editor who does not care to work in pastel,—to whom the blue pencil is taboo,—for he shall be held in honored re-membrance of all writers, and his end shall be peace."

" Amen!" said the Timid Aspirant.

XX

THE DIALECT STORE

I SUPPOSE I dreamed it; but if there is n't such a store, there might be, and it would help quill-drivers a lot," said the newspaper man, as he and his friend were waiting to give their order in a down-town restaurant yesterday noon.

"What store are you talking about, and what dream? Don't be so vague, old man," said his friend the magazine-writer.

"Why, a dialect store. Just the thing for you. I was walking down Fifth Avenue, near Twenty-first Street, and I saw the sign, 'Dialect shop. All kinds of dialects sold by the yard, the piece, or in quantities to suit.' I thought that maybe I might be able to get some Swe-

dish dialect to help me out on a little story
I want to write about Wisconsin, so I
walked in. The place looked a good deal
like a dry-goods store, with counters
down each side, presided over by some
twenty or thirty clerks, men and women.

" The floor-walker stepped up to me and
said, 'What can I do for you?' 'I want
to buy some dialect,' said I. 'Oh, yes;
what kind do you want to look at? We
have a very large assortment of all kinds.
There 's quite a run on Scotch just now;
perhaps you 'd like to look at some of
that.' 'No; Swedish is what I 'm after,'
I replied. 'Oh, yes; Miss Jonson, show
this gentleman some Swedish dialect.'

"I walked over to Miss Jonson's department, and she turned and opened a
drawer that proved to be empty. 'Are
you all out of it?' I asked. 'Ja; but I
skall have some to-morrer. A faller from
St. Paul he baen haer an' bought seventy
jards.'

"I was disappointed, but as long as I
was there I thought I 'd look around;
so I stepped to the next counter, behind

which stood a man who looked as if he had just stepped out of one of Barrie's novels. 'Have you Scotch?' said I. 'I hae joost that. What 'll ye hae? Hielan' or lowlan', reeleegious or profane? I 've a lairge stock o' gude auld Scotch wi' the smell o' the heather on it; or if ye 're wantin' some a wee bit shop-worn, I 'll let ye hae that at a lower price. There 's a quantity that Ian Maclaren left oot o' his last buke.' I expressed surprise that he had let any escape him, and he said: 'Hech, mon, dinna ye ken there 's no end to the Scots?' I felt like telling him that I was sorry there had been a beginning, but I refrained, and he went on: 'We 're gettin' airders fra the whole English-sp'akin' warld for the gude auld tongue. Our manager has airdered a fu' line of a' soorts in anticipation of a brisk business, now that McKinley—gude Scotch name, that—is President.'

"I should have liked to stay and see a lot of the Scotch, as it seemed to please the man to talk about his goods; but I wanted to have a look at all the dialects,

so I bade him good morning, and stepped
to the next department—the negro.

"Here an unctuous voice called out:
"'Fo' de Lawd! Ah don' b'lieve you 'll
pass me widout buyin'. Got 'em all
hyah, boss—Sou' Ca'lina an' Ten'see an'
Virginny. Tawmas Nelson Page buys a
heap er stuff right yer. Dat man sut'n'y
got a great haid. He was de fustes' one
ter see how much folks was dyin' ter git a
leetle di'lect er de ra'ht sawt, an' Ah
reckon Ah sol' him de fus' yard he evah
bo't.'

"'Do you sell it by the yard?' I asked,
just to bring him out. 'Shuah!' and
pulling down a roll of black goods, he un-
rolled enough dialect to color 'Uncle
Tom's Cabin.' But I said, 'I don't want
to buy, uncle; but I 'm obliged to you for
showing it to me.' 'Oh, dat 's all right,
boss. No trouble to show goods. Ah
reckon yo' nev' saw sech a heap er local
col'in' as dat. Hyah! hyah! hyah! We
got de goods, an' any tahm you want to
fix up a tale, an' put in de Queen's English in black, come yer an' as' fer me.

Good day, sah.'   And I passed on to the next—Western dialect.

"Here I found that James Whitcomb Riley had just engaged the whole output of the plant.   The clerk had an assistant in his little son,—a Hoosier boy,—and he piped up: 'We got 'ist a littul bit er chile's di'lec', an' my popper says 'at ef Mist' Riley don't come an' git it soon 'at I can sell it all my own se'f. 'At 'd be the mostest fun!' and his childish treble caused all the other clerks in the store to look around and smile kindly at him.

"In the German department the clerk told me he was not taking orders for dialect in bulk. 'Zome off dose tayatree-kalers dey buy it, aber I zell not de best to dem.   I zell imitation kints "made in Chairmany."   Aber I haf der best eef you vant it.'

"I told him I did not care to buy, and passed on to the French-Canadian department. The clerk was just going out to lunch; but although I told him I merely wished to look, and not to buy, he said politely: 'I try hall I can for get di'lect, but hup in Mon'réal dat McLennan he use hall dere is; but bymby I speak for some dat a frien' have, an' he sen' me some. An' 'e tell me I 'll get hit las' summer.'

I expressed a polite wish that he might get his goods even sooner than 'las' summer,' and walked to the Jew-dialect counter, over which I was nearly pulled by the Hebrew clerk. 'You 're chust in time,' he said. 'Say, veepin' Rachel! but I sell you a parkain. Some goots on'y been ust vun veek on der staich; unt so hellep me cracious! you look so like mein prudder Imre dat I let dem go '— here he lowered his voice to a whisper— 'I let dem go fer a qvarter uf a darler.'

"I resisted him, and hurried to the Yankee department. There was tall hustling going on there, and a perfect mob of buyers of all sorts and conditions of writers; and it took half a dozen men, women, and children, including three typical farmers, to wait on them; and they were selling it by the inch and by the carload. 'Wall, I 'm plumb tired. Wisht they 'd let up so 'st I could git a snack er somep'n' inside me,' said one; and he looked so worn out that I passed on to

the Irish counter. A twinkling-eyed young Irishman, not long over, in answer to my question, said: 'Sure, there 's not much carl fer larrge quantities av ut. Jane Barlow do be havin' a good dale, an' the funny papers do be usin' ut in smarl lots, but 't is an aisy toime I have, an' that 's a good thing, fer toimes is harrd.'

"I paused a moment at the English-dialect counter, and the rosy-cheeked clerk said: 'Cawn't I show you the very litest thing in Coster?' I told him no, and he offered me Lancashire and Yorkshire at 'gritely reduced rites'; but I was proof against his pleading, and having now visited all the departments but one, went to that."

"What was it?" asked the writer for the magazines.

"The tough-dialect counter."

"Tough is not a dialect," said he.

"Maybe not, but it sounds all right, all right. Well, whatever it is, the fellow in charge was a regular Ninth-Warder, and when I got abreast of him he hailed me with, 'Soy, cully, wot sort d' yer want? I got a chim-dandy Sunny-school line er samples fer use in dose joints, or I c'n gi' yer hot stuff up ter de limit an' beyon'. See? Here 's a lot of damaged "wot t' 'ells" dat I 'll trun down fer a fiver, an' no questions ast. Soy, burn me fer a dead farmer if I ever sol' dem at dat figger before; but dey 's some dat Townsen' did n' use, an' yet dey 's dead-sure winners wit' de right gang. See?'

"And then I woke up, if I was asleep; and if I was n't, I wish I could find the store again, for I 'd be the greatest dialect-writer of the age if I could get goods on credit there. Say, waiter, we came for lunch, not supper."

XXI

"FROM THE FRENCH"

WHEN a Frenchman sets out to write a tale that shall be wholly innocuous, he succeeds—and thereby drives his readers to seek in De Maupassant and Zola the antidote for his poisoning puerility.

He generally lays the scene in London, that he may air his ignorance of things foreign; and when the tale is done it contains absolutely nothing that would bring the blush of shame to any cheek in Christendom, seek said cheek where you might.

The following is a fair sample of the unharmful French story. I trust that if it had been printed without preamble or credit, the discerning reader would have

exclaimed, upon reading it, "From the
French!" I have called it—

IT IS GOOD TO BE GOOD

In the great city of London, which, as
you may know, is in England, there is a
bridge, famous throughout the whole town
as London Bridge. One dark night, many
years ago, two men started to cross it in
opposite directions, and running into each
other, their heads crashed together in the
fog which day and night envelops the city.

"*Parbleu!*" cried one, a fellow of in-
finite wealth; "but have you, then, no
better use for your head than to make of
it a battering-ram?"

"*Sapristi!*" replied the other, speaking
in the coarse tones of an English mechanic
out of work. "What matters it what I
do with it? A moment more and I shall
be in the Thames" (a large river corre-
sponding to our Seine, and in equal demand
by suicides). "To-night, for the first
time in my life, I commit suicide!"

"Why, then," said the other, "we will

7*

jump together, for it is for that purpose that I have come to this great bridge.".

"But," said the mechanic, "why should you commit suicide? I can tell by the feeling of your garments that you are rich, and by the softness of your head that you are noble."

"True, I am both of those things, but, also, I have exhausted every pleasure in life but the pleasure of suicide, and would now try that. But you, you are a mechanic out of work, as I can tell by your speech. Why should you seek pleasure instead of employment?"

"Alas, sir! I have at home one wife and seventeen children, all flaxen-haired, and all as poor as I. I cannot bear to go home to them without even the price of a *biftek* or a *rosbif*." ·

"Come," said the nobleman; "I will defer my sport for the night. I have never seen a starving family. It will furnish me with a new sensation."

"Ah! but you have a kind heart, and I will not refuse you. The river will keep. Follow me."

They followed each other through the region of the Seven Clocks, and through Blanc Chapel, afterward the scene of the murders of " Jean the RApper," until they came to the wretched apartment of the poor artisan. There, huddled in the corner of the room, were sixteen of the starving but still flaxen-haired children. The mother sat near the fireplace, so that she might be near the warmth when it came. In the other corner of the room— for they were so poor, these people, that they could not afford four corners—sat a

vision of beauty, aged seventeen and a girl, *ma foi!* At sight of her the count's eyes filled with tears of compassion, and he handed his purse to the wretched father and said: "My good man, do not stir from here. I will return in an hour with furniture! "

Tears of gratitude coursed down the thirty-eight cheeks of the poor family, and they no longer felt hungry, for they knew that in a short time they would be sitting upon real sofas and rocking in chairs like those they had seen through the windows of the rich on Holy Innocents' Day.

The count, whose full title was Sir Lord Ernold Cicil Judas Georges Herold Wallington, grandson of the great Lord of Wallington, was as good as his word, and in an hour he returned with six of his servants, bearing sofas and cushions and tables and tête-à-têtes, and what not.

The family seated themselves on the furniture, and, clasping his knees, overwhelmed him with thanks.

" *Dame! Sacré!* " cried he. " It is nothing, this thing I have done. What is it that it is? Know, then, that for the first time in my life I have the happiness." Then, turning to the father: " Give me the purse. I left it as a collateral. Now that you have the furniture, you will not need it. But that angelic being there, she shall never weep again. I will take her with me."

" Ah! " said the mother; " but that is like you, Count WAllington. You mean that she is to be a maid in your father's house? Ah! what prosperity!"

"Ah! do not insult the most beautiful being who ever went about in a London fog. She a servant? Never! I will make her my wife. She shall be Miledi Comptesse Ernold CIcil Judas Georges HErold WAllington!"

In Southwark-on-Trent, a suburb of London, is the hospital for those about to commit suicide. Ring the bell at the gate, and you will be admitted by sixteen flaxen-haired ones who will conduct you to the governor and matron. Need I say who they are, or whose money built the institution?

And when you read in London *Ponch*, among the court news, that a great beauty has been presented to the Queen of Eng-

land, London, and Ireland, you will know
that it is the Comptesse WAllington. She
is presented at all the levees, and, with
her husband, the handsome and philanthropic Lord WAllington, is the cynosure
of all English eyes.

It is good to be good.

XXII

ON THE VALUE OF DOGMATIC UTTERANCE

FROM MY "GUIDE TO YOUNG AUTHORS"

Y dear young reader, if you are thinking of launching a little craft upon the troublous sea of literature, see that it is well ballasted with dogmatic assertions. (I should like to continue this nautical metaphor further, but I am such a landlubber that I doubt if I should be able to mix it properly, and what interest has a metaphor if it be not well mixed?) But to continue in plain English: A dogmatic assertion carries conviction to the minds of most unthinking people—in other words, to most people. (You and I don't think, dear reader, and is it likely that we are worse than the rest of mankind?)

If you purpose becoming a novelist of character, follow my directions, and your first book will nail your reputation to the mast of public opinion. Fill your story full of such utterances as these: "Chaplain Dole always nodded his head a great many times to express affirmation. This is a common practice with persons who are a little hard of hearing." (It is n't, and yet it may be, for all I know to the contrary; but it will carry weight. Nine persons out of ten will say, "Why, that 's so, is n't it? Have n't you noticed it?")

It doesn't matter what you say; if you say it dogmatically it will go. Thus: "She walked with the slow, timid step that is so characteristic of English spinsters." That 's a fine one, for it may excite contradiction, and contradiction is advertisement. Here are half a dozen examples: "He tapped his forehead with his left little finger, a gesture peculiar to people who have great concentration of mind." "His half-closed eyes proclaimed

him a shrewd business man.   Why is it
that your keen man of affairs should always look out at the world through a slit?"
"The child spoke in that raucous tone
of voice that always presages cerebral
trouble."   "Miss de
Mure waved her fan
languidly,   with   a
scarcely   perceptible
wrist motion, a sure
indication that she was
about to capitulate, but
Mr. Wroxhaemme, not
being a keen observer,
took no note of it."
And, "He spoke but
three words, yet you
sensed that he was an
advocate.   Why is it
that a lawyer cannot
conceal his profession?

A doctor may talk all day, and if he bar
shop his vocation will not be detected;
but a lawyer tunes up his vocal chords, as
it were, and the secret is out."

If all the above specimens of "observa-

tion" were introduced into your story the
critics would unite in praising your keenness of vision.

Perhaps you would like to figure as a
musical author. Few authors know anything about music, and you don't have to;
dogmatism and alliteration in equal parts
will take the trick. Please step this way
(as they say in the stores) and I will show
you.

"She played Chopin divinely—but she
did not care to clean dishes. Chopin and
care of a house do not coalesce. A girl
may love Beethoven and yet busy herself
with baking; Bach and the Beatitudes are
not antagonistic; Haydn, Handel, and
housekeeping hunt together; Schumann
and Schubert are not incompatible with
sweetness and serenity of demeanor and a
love for sewing; Mozart and Mendelssohn
may be admired and the girl will also love
to mend stockings; Weber and work may
be twins: but Chopin and cooking, Wagner
and washing, Berlioz or Brahms and bast-
ing, Dvořák and vulgar employment—or
Dvořák and darning (according as you

pronounce Dvořák)—are eternally at war. So, when I have said that Carlotta was a devotee of Chopin, I have implied that her poor old mother did most of the housework, while the sentimental maiden coquetted with the keys continually."

Fill your stories with such bits of false observation, and ninety-nine persons out of a hundred will accept them at their face-value; which remark, being in itself a dogmatic assertion, will doubtless carry weight and conviction with it.

XXIII

THE SAD CASE OF DEACON PERKINS

IT is now some fifteen years since the dialect story assumed undue prominence in the literary output of the time, and about eight since it became a " craze." There is no craze without its attendant disease or ailment: thus roller-skating developed " roller's heel "; gum-chewing, " chewer's jaw "; bicycling, the " bicycle face," and later the " leg "; housekeeping, " housemaid's knee "; golf-playing, " idiocy "; and so on, every craze having a damaging effect upon some portion of the anatomy. It is only within the last year, however, that it has been discovered that an over-indulgence in dialect stories is liable to bring on an affection of the tongue.

A peculiarly sad case and the most notable that has thus far been brought to the attention of the public is that of Deacon Azariah Perkins of West Hartford, Connecticut.

Far from deploring the spread of the dialect story, he reveled in it, reading all the tales that he could get hold of in magazines or circulating library. But his was not a healthy, catholic taste; he had ears and eyes for one dialect alone—the negro. For him Ian Maclaren and Barrie spread their most tempting Scotch jaw-breakers in vain; he had no desire for them. After fifteen years of negro dialect in every form in which Southern and Northern writers can serve it, any specialist in nervous disorders could have told the deacon that he was liable to have " negromania "; but West Hartford does not employ specialists, and so the stroke came unheralded, with all the suddenness of apoplexy.

Deacon Perkins has always been able to

think standing; indeed, he has been called the Chauncey Depew of West Hartford, and no revival meeting or strawberry fes-

tival or canned clam-bake was considered a success unless the deacon's ready tongue took part in the exercises.

Last Sunday they had a children's festival in the Congregational Church, and after the children had made an end of reciting and singing, the deacon was called upon for a few remarks. He is a favorite with young and old, and a man of great purity and simplicity of character. He arose with alacrity and walked down the isle with the lumbering gait peculiar to New-Englanders who have struggled with rocky farms the best part of their lives. He ascended the platform steps, inclined his head to the audience, and spoke as follows:

"Mah deah li'l' chillun! Yo' kahnd sup'inten'ent has ast me to mek a few re-mahks." (Subdued titters on the part of the scholars.) "Ah don' s'pose you-all 'll b'lieve me w'en Ah say dat Ah too was once a li'l' piccaninny same as yo', but Ah was, an' Ah 'membeh how mah ol' mammy use teh tek me to Sunny-school." (Consternation on the part of the superinten-dent and teachers.)

"Now, ef you-all wan' to go to heb'n w'en yo' die, be ci'cumspectious 'bout de observence ob de eighth c'man'ment. Hit ain't so awful wicked ter steal—dat ain't hit, but hit 's jes nach'ly tryin' to a man's self-respec' ter git cotched. Don' steal jes fer deviltry, but ef yo' is 'bleeged ter steal, study de wedder repohts, ac' accord-in', an'—don' git foun' out—or in, eiver."

During the delivery of this remark-
able speech the deacon's face wore his
habitual expression; a kindly light shone
in his eye, a smile of ineffable sweetness
played about his lips, and he evidently
imagined that he was begging them to
turn from their evil ways and seek the
narrow path.

But at this juncture Dr. Pulcifer of
New York, the eminent neurologist, who
happened to be spending Sunday in West
Hartford, whispered to the superintendent,
and on receiving an affirmative nod to his
interrogation, went up to the platform.
He held out his hand to Deacon Perkins,
who was making a rhetorical pause, and
said kindly, "Good morning, uncle."

"Mornin', sah," said the deacon, bowing awkwardly and scratching his head.

"Can you direct me to a good melon-
patch?"

Deacon Perkins gave vent to an unctuous negro chuckle. Then, holding up his
forefinger to enjoin caution, he tiptoed
off the platform, closely followed by the
doctor; and before nightfall he was on

his way to a private hospital for nervous diseases, where rest and a total abstention from negro-dialect stories is expected to restore him to his usual sane condition of mind in a short time.

XXIV

THE MISSING-WORD BORE

THEN, there 's that bore whose thoughts come by freight, and the freight is always late. You know what 's coming, that is, you can imagine the way-bill, but he won't let you help him to make better time, and runs his train of thought as if it were on a heavy grade.

He starts to tell a story, blinking his red eyes, meanwhile, as if he thought that they supplied the motive power for his tongue. To make listening to him the harder, he generally tells a very old story.

"One day, William Makepeace—er—er—"

"Thackeray," you say, intending to help him. Of course it is Thackeray, and he was going to tell about the novelist and the Bowery boy; but he is so pig-headed that he shifts on to another track.

"No; Dickens, Charles Dickens.   One day, when Charles Dickens was at work on 'Bleak'—er—er—"

"'Bleak House'?" you say.

"No!" he snaps; "'Dombey and Son.' One day, when Charles Dickens was at work on 'Dombey and Son,' he was approached by his biographer, John—er—er—"

"Forster?"

"No; it wasn't his biographer, either; it was Edmund Yates."

You now take a gleeful pleasure in seeing how hopelessly you can make him tangle himself up by the refusal of your help, but he does n't care.

He 'll tell it in his own words, though the heavens fall and though he starts a hundred stories.

"Charles Dickens had a very loud way of—er—er—"

"Dressing?"

"No, no!   He had a loud way of talking, and he and Edmund—er—er—"

"Yates?"

"No, sir; Edmund Spenser."

Of course this is arrant nonsense on the face of it, but he won't admit that he 's made pi of his story, and he goes on:

"Edmund said that Charles—"

"Dickens?"

"No, sir; Charles Reade.   Edmund said that Charles Reade thought George —er—"

"Meredith?"

"No; hang it all!   George Eliot.   He thought that George Eliot never wrote a better book than 'Silas'—er—"

"'Marner'?"

"Not at all!   'Silas Lapham.'"

Now, if you are merciful, or if you are refinedly cruel, either one, you will allow him to finish his story in peace, and, like as not, he will start all over again by saying: "I guess I inadvertently got hold of the wrong name at the beginning. It was not Dickens, as you said, but Thackeray. Thackeray was one day walking along the Bowery when he met a typical—" And so on to the bitter end.

For the sake of speed, do not ever interrupt his kind!

XXV

THE CONFESSIONS OF A CRITIC

I MET a prominent literary critic the other evening. A review signed with his name or even with his initials is apt to make or mar the work treated therein.

Now, I have not a little hypnotic power, and the mischievous idea came into my head to hypnotize him and make him " confess."

We were sitting in the reading-room of an up-town club. I led the conversation to the subject of hypnotism, and soon gained the critic's consent to be put into a trance.

I did not influence him any more than to put his mind in the attitude of truthfully answering what questions I might ask him.

Q. Which do you prefer to criticize, a book that has already been reviewed or one that is perfectly fresh?

A. Oh, one that has been reviewed, and the oftener the better. I thus gain some idea of the trend of critical opinion and shape my review accordingly.

Q. Do you ever run counter to the general sentiment?

A. Yes; if I find that a book has been damned with faint praise, I sometimes laud it to the skies and thus gain a reputation for independence that is very useful to me. Or if a book has been heralded by the best critics of both countries as "the book of the year," I sometimes pick it to pieces, taking its grammar as a basis, or some other point that I think I can attack without injury to my reputation for discernment, and again I score a victory for my independence.

Q. Why don't you like to be the first to review a new book?

A. For the same reason that most critics hate to—unless, indeed, they are just out of college and are cock-sure of everything. I fear that its author may be one of the numerous coming men. I may be entirely at sea about the book. I prefer to get some idea of what the con-census of the best opinion is.

Q. Then you do not consider your own the best opin-ion?

A. No; no one critic's opinion is worth much.

Q. Can you tell an author by his style?

A. Always, if I know who he is before I begin to read. But it is hazardous work to say such-and-such a work is by such-and-such a man unless there are internal evidences aside from the style. Once a book was sent to me for criticism. Before I opened it I lent it to a waggish friend of mine, and he returned it next day. I looked at the title-page, saw that it was by an absolutely unknown man and that the

scene was laid in India, and, of course, I
felt safe in giving it fits on the principle
that Rudyard Kipling is not likely to be
equaled in this generation as a depicter
of Indian life. Well, I said that it was
painfully crude and amateurish; that it
might do for the "Servants' Own," but
was not a book for ladies and gentlemen;
that it had absolutely no style or local coloring; that the scene might as well have
been laid in Kamchatka; and that it was
marked by but one thing, audacity, for the
author had borrowed some of Kipling's
characters—to the extent of the names
only. In short, I had fun with that book,
for I knew that my fellow-critics would
with one accord turn and rend it. By
mere chance I did n't sign it.

Q. And who had written the book?

A. Why, Kipling. My friend had cut
another name out of a book and had pasted
it so neatly over Kipling's wherever his
occurred that I was, of course, taken un-
awares. You can't bank on style. Look
how positive people were Mark Twain had
not written " Jeanne d'Arc."

I here interrupted the flow of his conversation to say : " Your experience is not
unlike that of the reviewer who criticized
' Silas Lapham,' and who had a sort of hazy
notion from the similarity of titles that it
was by the author of ' Silas Marner.'   You
may remember, it created a good deal of
amusement at the time.   He said that it
was a mistake for George Eliot to try
to write a novel of American life; that.
the vital essence—American humor—was
lacking; that Silas Lapham was a dull
Englishman transplanted bodily into a
very British Boston; that his daughters
were mere puppets, and the attempts at
Americanisms doleful in the extreme.
He concluded by saying that her ' Romola '
had shown that she was best on British
soil, and that she would better keep to the
snug little isle in the future."

"Yes," said he, with a grin; " I remember that.   It was my first criticism.
Most people supposed it was a humorous
skit, even the editors who accepted it, but
I never was more in earnest.   I was young
then."

Q. If you received a book to review with the name of Hardy on the title-page, would you give it a good send-off?

A. I certainly should, for I am a great admirer of Hardy; but I should prefer to wait until some one else had done so, for fear it might be another put-up job and turn out to be the work of some fifth-rate English author.

I then brought him out of his trance. He sat silent for a moment. I picked up the "Saturday Review" from the table and said, "Criticism is a very noble calling."

"It is indeed," he responded earnestly. "It is one that requires great insight into human nature, absolute independence, and not a little charity."

With which beautiful sentiments he rose and, bowing, left the room.

XXVI

HOW 'RASMUS PAID THE MORTGAGE

A DIALECT STORY

I

Oh, de wolf an' de har' dey had a great fight.
   (Down on de ribber de wil' geese is callin'.)
De har' pulled de wolf's teeth so 's he could n' bite.
   (A-callin' me to my long home !)
Said de wolf to de har', " Don' hit so hard."
   (De dew on de hollyhock 's all a-dryin' !)
An' he killed de har' w'en he co't him oaf his guard.
   (Ah 'll dry up an' go home !)

UP the vista formed by a narrow, tortuous Virginia lane, came Uncle 'Rasmus, an aged darky, singing one of the songs of his race that never grow old—because they die young, it may be.

As he hobbled along the path, he talked to himself, as was his wont:

"Golly! Ah mus' hurry up, o' de fo'kses won' hab no dinnah; for, be jabers, 't is mesilf that has got to git riddy dthat same. Och, worra! worra! but 't is no synekewer Oi 'm havin', an' dthat 's dther trut'."

Just then his watch struck five minutes to six, and he ran off toward the homestead of Squire Lamar, saying, as he did so, in his quaint way: "Veepin' Rachel! der boss will kick der live out mit me."

Before the war Squire Lamar had been the richest man in Oconee County; but the conflict had ruined him, and he now had little except his plantation, horses, and stables. He lived in his ancestral house, which was heavily mortgaged, with his wife and children.

'Rasmus, his only servant, an ex-slave, supported the family by collecting dollars —at night.

As he ran toward the house, he saw Squire Lamar on the veranda. Just then a horseman dashed up. He was the sheriff of Oconee County. 'Rasmus took

9

advantage of the commotion, and ran into the kitchen to cook the dinner. On seeing the squire, the sheriff called out to him: "The mortgage on this place will be foreclosed if the $3600 due is not forthcoming by to-morrow noon."

"Alas!" said the squire; "you see how we are situated. I have n't a dollar, and would n't know how to earn one if I had."

At this juncture, 'Rasmus, who had cooked the dinner during the conversation, came up and said: "Massa, Ah 's a free man, Ah know Ah is; but avick, 't is a mighty shmall wan Oi 'd be if I would n't help out a poor omadhaun like yerself. 'Caed mille fail the Bryn Mawr dolce far niente.' Zat ees mon motto, an' so, deah massah, I will guarantee to git de money by to-morrow noon." Then turning to the sheriff, he said in a manly tone that contrasted ill with his ragged garments: "Ye maun fash awee, laddie, doon the skim."

After a few more words, the sheriff, who was really a kind man at heart, rode off, saying he would be on hand the next day, and if the money were not forthcoming, he would march them all off to the county jail, ten miles distant. After blowing the dinner-horn, 'Rasmus hobbled off to his humble cottage.

II

ON arriving at his cabin, 'Rasmus took a bolster-case full of dollars from under the bed, and proceeded to count them. There were just $3000. "Now, Ah mus' git $600 more before to-morrow, or else me poor masther 'll be wor-r-rkin' in the chain-gang. Ach, Himmel!" said the good old darky, his eyes suffused with tears, "if dot took blace, it zeems as if mein herz would break."

He calmly decided on a plan of action, however. Waiting until night had flung over the earth a pall, through which the silvery moon cast shimmering beams aslant the quivering aspens of the forest, and the snoring of the birds told him that nature slept, he left his house and walked briskly off to the highway.

About that time a lawyer was riding along the road on horseback, with a wallet

containing a share of an estate worth $600, which he had secured for an old woman.

'Rasmus saw the traveler, saw the horse, saw the wallet.

The traveler saw no one. He was blind—drunk.

'Rasmus cut a stout bludgeon.

The traveler ambled on.

'Rasmus clasped the bludgeon.

The traveler continued to amble.

'Rasmus stole up beside him. . . .

The traveler lay in the ditch.

'Rasmus jumped on the horse, the wallet in his hand, and galloped home, stabling the beautiful animal in his cabin to avoid being suspected of the murder.

Placing his shoe in front of the one window of the cabin, that none might see him, he counted the money, and found it amounted to just $600, which, together with the $3000, formed the sum required by the sheriff. This made him so happy that he picked up a banjo and played Wagner's "Götterdämmerung" through once or twice, accompanying himself on his throat in a rich tenor. He then turned out the gas and retired, to sleep as only a good, unselfish soul can.

9*

III

IT is 11:45 A. M. The squire and his family, who have heard nothing from 'Rasmus, are on the veranda, anxiously awaiting the arrival of the sheriff.

11:50 A. M.! Is 'Rasmus dead? Has the sheriff relented?

11:55. Good lack! The sheriff is seen galloping toward the house, and yet there is no sign of 'Rasmus.

That individual, who is nothing if not dramatic, is sitting behind the house on horseback, awaiting the stroke of twelve.

The door of the ormolu cuckoo-clock in the kitchen opens, the cuckoo advances. At her first note the sheriff jumps from his horse; at the second he walks sternly upon the veranda; at the third he asks for the money; at the fourth and fifth they tell him that 'Rasmus has disappeared; at the sixth, seventh, and eighth he handcuffs them all together; at the ninth, tenth, and eleventh he jumps on his horse and rides off, dragging them behind

him; and at the twelfth 'Rasmus trots
leisurely out from behind the house, and,
opening a carpet-bag, counts out $3600
in silver!

The astonished sheriff puts the money
into his pocket, gives Squire Lamar a re-
ceipt in full for it, unlocks the handcuffs,
and the family resume their wonted places
on the veranda.

But all was not yet done. 'Rasmus
still had his bludgeon with him, and a few
deft strokes on the sheriff's head were all-
sufficient. 'Rasmus then took back the
money and gave it to Squire Lamar.
Then he told them all to remain perfectly
still, and whistling three times, an amateur
photographer made his appearance, ad-
justed his apparatus, and took their pic-
tures.

Sarony could have wished for no better
subjects. On the broad veranda lay
the old lady prone on the floor, reading
the " Tallahassee Inland Mariner "; at her
side sat her daughter, Turk-fashion, shel-
ling a pea; while the son and heir reclined
near by, reading an account by a Prussian

officer of the third battle of Bull Run. The father, weighted down with dollars, snored in the background.

And beaming on them all with the consciousness of having done his best and done it well, old 'Rasmus stood, singing ventriloquially, so as not to injure the picture, this negro plantation song:

> De ribber Jordan I can see,
>   Toujour jamais, toujour jamais;
> Mein liebe frau, ach, she lofes me,
>   Fair Jeannie het awa!
> Then I wen' daown the caows to milk,
>   Toujour jamais, toujour jamais;
> Me lika banan' as softa as silk,
>   Helas, cordon, by gar!

XXVII

'MIDST ARMED FOES

BY THE AUTHOR OF "DUNN TO DEATH;
OR, THE WEATHER PROPHET'S FATE,"
"SARAH THE SALES-WOM-LADY; OR,
FROM COUNTER TO COUNTESS," ETC.

RAOUL CHEVREUILLY stood within a rude hut in the dark recesses of the forest of Fontainebleau. By his side stood his lady-love, the beautiful Perichole Perihelion. Without, the night was black and the wind roared as it is wont to do in stories of this type.

"Dost fear aught, my precious?" asked Raoul, gazing at the French face of the lovely Parisian.

"Why should I fear when I am pro-

tected by my Raoul—how do you pronounce Raoul, anyway?" replied she.

"I long ago gave up trying. But,
Perichole, while I would not have you fear,
yet it is no light task that I have under-
taken—your defense against as fierce a
pack of roistering thieves as ever beset
the forest and who now surround this
hut. Let but the wind die down so that
they may be heard, and they will hurl ex-
ecrations at me and beat down the door.
Réné Charpentier seeks my life because I
have promised to be yours, or rather because you have promised to be mine.
But he shall kill me only at the expense
of my life. Yea, though he had twice a
hundred myrmidons at his back and beck."

For answer the entrancing girl took a
mother-of-pearl jews' harp off the wall and
played "Mlle. Rosie O'Grady," "There 'll
be a chaud temps in the vieux ville ce
soir," and other simple French ditties.

Instead of admiring her pluck, Raoul
was moved to fury, and he cried in French,
—this whole business is supposed to be in
French, except the descriptions,—"Is it

impossible to move you to a realization of my bravery? Know, then, that, save for ourselves, there is not a human being within three miles of this hut. I had thought that you would be moved to added love by such an exhibition of bravery on my part as your defense against a hundred bravos; but, *viol di gamba!* you have no imagination."

" And Réné Charpentier? "

" There is no such fellow. He is but a pigment—I mean figment of my brain."

Flinging a pair of arms around his French neck, the adorable Perichole kissed Raoul again and once more. Then she said, " My adored one, that you were brave I suspected—are you not the hero of a French novel? But I never knew that you were such a lovely liar.   Raoul, my own forevermore!"

And her beautiful face beamed with a love-light whose wick had been newly trimmed.

XXVIII

AT THE SIGN OF THE CYGNET

A COSMOPOLITAN ROMANCE

I

IT was late spring in New England. Buttercups bespangled the grass and nodded and smiled at the apple-blossoms in the trees. And the apple-blossoms nodded in return, and in a few days fluttered down to the buttercups.

On the front stoop of an old baronial castle in the south of France stood Armand Maria Sylvestre de Faience Pomade Pommedeterre. He had been standing there all the morning, he knew not why. True, he looked well, but he would have looked as well anywhere else, and he might have been doing something. Still, there is time. It is but the first chapter.

Godiva Churchill Churchill, of Churchill Wolde, Biddecumb on Baddecumb, the only daughter of her widowed mother and widowered father, cantered slowly down the roadway that led to Churchill Hall, the home of the Churchills for seven centuries. Her right cheek was over-flushed, and ever and anon she bit her chin. England could boast of no prettier girl than Godiva, nor did England boast of it as much as Godiva did.

II

IT is summer in New England. The as yet color-less spears of gold-enrod give warning that the year is speeding speedily.

The buttercups fled long ago with the apple-blossoms, and from the verdant limbs of the apple-trees hang bullet-like apples.

Armand Maria Sylvestre de Faience Pomade Pommedeterre is still in the south of France. My French map is mislaid, and I cannot spell the name of the place he is at, but it is on bottles, I think. He has left the front stoop, and passes his time gazing at the goldfish in the fountain and waiting to be drawn into the plot of my story. Patient man!

Godiva Churchill Churchill, of Churchill Wolde, Biddecumb on Baddecumb, is still in the saddle, filled with vague longings.

III

PURPLE asters fringe the highways of New England, and rosy apples depend from the boughs in countless orchards. (I think that scenery is my strong point.)

Armand Maria Sylvestre de Faience Pomade Pommedeterre is chafing at my delay, but continues to reside in the south of France from sheer inertia.

Godiva Churchill Churchill, of Churchill Wolde, Biddecumb on Baddecumb, has worn out the left fore foot of her horse by her incessant cantering upon the graveled paths of Churchill Hall.   She is beginning to feel resentment at me for the enforced monotony of her existence, but heavens! how can I help it?   I 'm trying my level best to evolve a plot.

IV

THE flowers that gladdened the meads and highways and shady lanes of New England are gone.   Winter's robes of office are thrown carelessly over the land-scape, and apples in innumerable barrels stand in the cellars, waiting for better prices.

The reason why I have so faithfully described New England scenery is because that 's the only kind of scenery I know anything about.

I am ashamed to confess it, but this is the last chapter, and blamed if I can think of any good reason for the departure of·

Armand Maria Sylvestre de Faience Pomade Pommedeterre from the south of France. He can't speak a word of English, and if you 're thinking of Godiva, she can't speak a syllable of French.

Poor Godiva Churchill Churchill, of Churchill Wolde, Biddecumb on Baddecumb! She is quite lame from her long-continued exercise in the saddle, but still canters aimlessly about. She has become the laughing-stock of all the tenants of Churchill Wolde, and it 's all my fault.

If she saw Armand she 'd fall in love with him, but I can't think of a way to bring about their meeting. That 's what it is to lack invention.

Just imagine me trying to write a novel!

Anyhow, I 've got a good title for the story.

THE END

XXIX

A SCOTCH SKETCH

THE shadows lengthened on old Ben Nevis. Surely none of my readers imagines that Ben Nevis is the hero of my simple Scotch sketch. If so, he is awa off. Ben Nevis is a mountain, and I have flung it in as a suitable background for the following conversation:

" Mither, mither, ye 'll mek nae doot o' haein' roast beef fer supper," said Hillocks Kilspindie, as he sat on the old bench in front of their cottage door.

With a troubled look, his mother, old Margaret Kilspindie, replied: " Man, Hillocks, div ye no see me buyin' the haggis ? "

" Yes, mither; but I 'm sair sick o' haggis. Syne Scotch literatoor kem in it 's hard put we are to live at all. I say may the plague take Maclaren and Barrie and Crockett. Before they began to write"—and in his excitement Hillocks was using as good English as any other Scotchman in real life—" roast beef and wheat bread and chops and tomato-sauce and other Christian dishes were good enough for us all. Then came the influx of Americans who wanted to see the scenes made immortal by the 'Bonnie Brier Bush' (I wish Ian might have scratched his writing-hand upon it) and the 'Window in Thrums' (which I wish some one had broken before Barrie saw it), and now it is haggis in the morning, and haggis at noon, and haggis at night, and Scotch dialect that tears my tongue to pieces all the time."

" Hech, my bairnie; but thae are wrang words, an' fu' o' unchristian bitterness."

"Oh, mother! drop your 'hechs' and your 'fu's.' There are no Americans about this evening. It 's hard enough to talk the abominable gibberish when we have to, without keeping it up all the time. But, tell me, mother, could n't you smuggle in a little roast beef to-night, and let me eat in the cellar?" And a pleading look came into the young man's eyes that was hard to resist.

"My bairn—I mean my boy, I 'd like to, but I dare not. Maclaren's inspectors are due here any minute, and I could ill afford to pay the heavy fine that would be levied if we were found with as English a thing as roast beef in the house. No, lad, we maun stick to parritch and haggis—I mean we must stick to oatmeal and haggis."

Just then the sentry that was stationed at the outskirts of the village to warn the villagers of the approach of Americans gave the laugh of warning: "H-O! H-O! H-O!" And, with a bitter look on his face, and a shake of his fist in the direction of Loch Lomond, Ben Nevis, Ben Bolt, and various other bits of Scotch scenery that were scattered about, Hillocks Kilspindie said to his mother: "Weel, as surees deith a' c'u'dna help it; tae be sittin' on peens for mair than twa oors, tryin' tae get a grup o' a man's heads. (I

learned that this morning, mother. Is n't
it a looloo?)"

"(Indeed it is, my son. Look out!
The Americans are almost within ear-shot.)

Noo we 've tae begin an' keep it up till
they gang awa, for there mauna be a
cheep aboot the hoose, for Annie's sake!
Here they are."

"Mither! Mither! if ye lo'e me bring
me mair haggis."

10*

CHORUS OF AMERICANS. Oh, how adorably Scotch!

" Losh keep us a', but the childie 'll eat his mither oot o' hoose an' hame wi' his haggis.   Ye 'll find some o' it i' the cupboard."

AMERICAN (*politely to* HILLOCKS). Have some haggis on me.

HILLOCKS (*with a canny Scotch leer*). Thanks; but I prefer a plate.

UNRELATED STORIES—RELATED

XXX

EPHRATA SYMONDS'S DOUBLE LIFE

I

EPHRATA SYMONDS was a knave. Of that there was no doubt. It stuck out all over him. His face was a chart of wickedness, and it was his open boast that he had never done any good in his life, and, please the devil, he never intended doing any. He had married early in life (in a fit of absent-mindedness), but he had long since forsaken his wife and children.

"Satan finds some mischief still for idle hands to do"; but, to speak in a paradox, Satan never gave him any employment, for he was ever busy—at evil. It was when he was just turned fifty that he was elected a member of the Evil-doers' Club. He soon became popular, and upon the incarceration of the president of the club, the trusted cashier of the Tyninth National Bank, Symonds was unanimously elected president in his place.

That he was the right man for the position he immediately proved by presenting the club with a fine new club-house, which he assured them was not his to give, or he would not have presented it. In the first six months of his presidency he eloped with two married women at once, and so  managed the trip that neither suspected that she was not quite alone in his company. He deserted them both in the West, and returned to pose before his fellow club-members. He diverted to his use the little property of a friendless woman, and in many characteristic ways showed himself to be thoroughly bad.

It was at this period of his life that his death came, and his last words were: " I am thankful that no man is the better for my having lived."

His fellow Evil-doers mourned his departure with sincerity. They felt that in losing such a thoroughly bad man they had suffered a loss which it would be impossible to repair. As the secretary feelingly put it," Hell is the worse for having him." " Yes," said another; " he was admirably bad. And it is the more to his credit that he was bad in spite of adverse influences. His parents were pious people, and Ephrata had every temptation to lead a life of virtue; but in the face of all the obstacles that his father put in the way of his becoming vicious, he persevered, and yesterday I had the honor of telling his old mother that her son was undoubtedly the most wicked man in New York. It made quite an impression on her. We shall ne'er see his like again."

The parlors of the Evil-doers' Club were draped in black, and mock resolutions of sympathy were sent to his deserted wife.

II

GREAT was the chagrin of the members of the club when it began to be bruited among them that Symonds had been leading a double life; that his wickedness was but a cloak to hide his goodness. The rumors were at first pooh-poohed, but when it was remembered that every third week he had always absented himself from town, the story that he was really a good man began to wear an air of truth. Detectives were set to work, and the damning proofs of his deceitful goodness multiplied rapidly, and at last the facts came out, but only to the club-members. They felt that it would not be creditable to allow such scandalous stories to be repeated to the world at large, which would only too willingly point the finger of scorn at them on learning that their chief officer had, in spite of every lure, gone right. Some might even go so far as to insinuate that maybe other members were better than they seemed to be.   No; Symonds's disreputable goodness should continue to be as well cloaked as he had cloaked it while alive.

The story of his goodness is as follows: It seems that every third week of his life had been spent in Boston, and while there he had earned a large income as a life-insurance agent.   It was his wont to spend this money in doing good.   Nothing was known in the Hub of his private life.   He lived at the Adams House, and cultivated an austerity of manner that repelled people; but by underhand means he contrived to ameliorate a deal of misery.

Having become convinced in his early youth that unostentatious benevolence was preferable to a life of good works blazoned forth to an admiring world, he had habituated himself to every form of vice, in order, under cover of it, to pursue unobserved the efforts he was to put forth for the good of his fellow-men.   And he had well succeeded.   When Elias Hapgood, who had for thirty years subsisted on the bounty of an unknown benefactor, read in the Boston "Herald" an account of the death of Ephrata Symonds, "the wickedest man in New York," he breathed a prayer of thankfulness that the world was rid of such a man, little knowing that he was misjudging his best friend. And Elias was but one of scores that had been similarly benefited. Symonds's charities had been literally endless and invariably anonymous. And now, after having, as it were, lived down his good works, it was a little hard that death should have torn from him the lifelong mask of deceit, and set him before his fellow-members for what he was—a thoroughly good man.

III

IT was a special business meeting of the Evil-doers' Club. The chairman rapped for order, and the secretary read the following resolutions:

"WHEREAS, It has pleased Nature to take from among us Ephrata Symonds, for some time our honored president;

"WHEREAS, We had always supposed him to be a man of the most exemplary wickedness, a man before whom all Evil-doers might well hide their diminished heads in despair of ever approaching his level of degradation;

"WHEREAS, His life had always seemed to us a perfectly unbroken and singularly consistent chain of crimes and enormities to be emulated by us all; and

"WHEREAS, It has lately come to be known that his wickedness was but a mask to hide a life of well-doing, occupied in its every third week with deeds of kindness and generosity;

"Therefore be it *Resolved*, That we, as members of this club, have been most shamefully imposed upon;

"*Resolved*, That we hereby express our contempt for a man who, with every incentive to be always bad, should have so far forgotten himself as to lead a third of a worthy life."

The secretary had not finished reading the resolutions when a messenger brought in a letter which he handed to the chairman as the clock pointed to eight fifty-eight.

It ran in this fashion:

FELLOW-MEMBERS: It is, by the time of reading this, probably plain to you that you have been taken in by me, and that, so far from my really having been a wicked person, I was a credit to my race and time.

True to my desire that to the rest of the world I should be accounted a bad man, I have caused to be delivered with this letter a box. It works its purpose at nine o'clock. Sit where you are and do not attempt to escape. The secret of my goodness rests, and shall rest, with you.

Yours insincerely, EPHRATA SYMONDS.

As the chairman finished reading he glanced at the clock. It was on the stroke of nine! He seized the box, and with a wild cry attempted to throw it through the window, but it was too late. A whirring noise was heard, followed by a terrific explosion, that left of club-house and -members naught save a hole in the ground.

Symonds's culpable goodness remained unknown to the world.

XXXI

A STRANGER TO LUCK

WHEN I got off the train at Darby-
ville, which, as all will remember,
is the junction of the L. M. & N.
and O. P. & Q. railroads, and found that,
owing to an accident, it would be an hour
before the train came in on the latter road,
I was vexed. Although ordinarily my
own thoughts are agreeable companions,
yet events of the past week, in which my
good judgment had not borne a conspicuous part, made it likely that for the nonce
these thoughts of mine would be more or
less unpleasant, and so I cast about for
some human nature to study.

At one end of the platform three or four
farmers were seated upon trunks. They

were alert-looking men, and, like me, were waiting for the train. As I neared them, one of their number, a tall, lanky, sharp-boned, knife-featured fellow, imperturbably good-natured-looking, and with an expression of more than ordinary intelligence in his eyes, left them and sauntered off down the road with long, irregular strides.

It was one of those calm, clear, dry days when sounds carry well, and although I did not join them, yet I heard every word of the conversation. Indeed, as their glances from time to time showed, they were not averse to having an auditor.

"It 's cur'us," said one of them, a ruddy-faced man with a white beard, "how unlucky a man c'n be an' yit manage to live." His eyes followed the shambling figure that had just left them. "I 'll help myself to some of thet terbacker, Jed. Left mine to hum, an' I have the teethache—awful." This to a short, stout man with a smooth face, who had just taken a liberal mouthful of tobacco from a paper that he drew from his hip-pocket.

"He'p 'se'f!" said the one addressed. Then he added, "Meanin' Seth, I s'pose?"

"Yes," replied the other. "I b'lieve thet ef Seth was to hev anythin' really fort'nit happen to him, it would throw him off his balance."

"'N' yit ther' never was a feller thet better deserved good luck than Seth. Most obligin' man I ever saw. Ain't no fool, nuther," remarked the third and last member of the group, a typical Uncle Sam in appearance, with prominent front teeth, and a habit of laughing dryly at everything that he or any one else said.

"He don't suffer fer the actooal needs of life, doos he?" asked the stout man whom the others called Jed.

"No—óh, no," answered Sam (for it turned out that so the typical Yankee was called). "No; he gits enough to eat and wear, but he never hez a cent to lay by, and never will."

"Don't drink, doos he?" asked Jed, who seemed to belong to a different town from the one wherein the others and Seth abode. His acquaintance with the one under discussion was evidently by no means intimate.

"No; he ain't got no vices 't I know of. Jes' onlucky."

"It 's s'prisin' haow tantalizin'ly clus good fortin hez come to him—different times," said the one who had asked for the tobacco, and whom the others called Silas.

"You 're *right*, Silas," assented Sam. "He c'n come nearer to good luck 'thout techin' it 'an any man I ever see."

"Don't seem to worrit him much," said Jed. "He seems cheerful."

"Don't nothin' worrit *him*," Sam continued. "Most easy-goin' man on the face of the airth. *He* don't ask fer sympathy. He takes great doses of bad luck 's ef 't was good fer his health."

"Never fergit," said Silas, "the time when he bought a fine new milch Jarsey at auction fer five dollars. Why, he hed two offers fer her nex' day, an' I *know* one of 'em was forty dollars—"

"Well, naow I call that purty lucky," interrupted Jed.

"Wait!" continued Silas, seating him-

self more comfortably on a trunk. "Seth
he would n't sell. Said he never did hev
his fill of milk, an' he was goin' to keep
her. Very nex' day, b' George! she
choked on a turnip, an' when
he faound her she was cold.
Man sympathized with him.
'Too bad, Seth,' says he;
'ye 'r' aout forty dollars.'
'Five 's all I figger it at,'
says Seth. 'Did n't *keer* to
sell.'

"Closest call 'at fortune
ever made him was time his
uncle Ralzemon aout West
died and left him $5000.
Everybody was glad, fer
every one likes Seth. I was
with him when he got the
letter f'om the lawyer
sayin' it was all in gold,
an' hed be'n expressed to him, thet bein'
one of the terms of the will. Mos' shif'-
less way of sendin' it, I thought," declared
Silas, compressing his lips. "'What ye
goin' to do with it, Seth?' says I. 'Put

11*

it in the bank?' 'Ain't got it yit,' says
he; 'an', what 's more, I never will.'
'Why d' ye think so?' says I. 'On
gin'al principles,' says he, a-laafin'.

"Sure 'nough, a few days later it was
printed in the paper thet a train aout in
Wisconsin hed be'n held up by robbers.
I was in the post-office when I saw it in
the paper, an' Seth was there too. 'Bet
ye a cooky thet my $5000 was on thet
train,' says he. 'Won't take ye,' says I;
'fer I 'll bet ye five dollars 't was, myse'f.'
'I 'll take ye,' says he. B' George! he
lost the five and the $5000 too, fer '*t was*
on the train, an' they never could git a
trace of it. The robbers hed took to the
woods, an' they never found 'em."

"Well, I swan!" ejaculated Jed, chew-
ing hard, and regarding with ominous look
a knot-hole in the platform.

Silas continued: "I says, 'I 'm sorry
fer ye, Seth.' Says he: 'I ain't no poorer
'an I was before I heard he 'd left it to
me.'"

"He was aout the five dollars he bet,
though," said Jed.

"Wa' n't, nuther," said Silas, rather shamefacedly. "I told him thet the bet was off."

"Why did n't he sue the comp'ny?" asked Jed.

"'At 's what I advised him doin', but he said 't wa' n't no use."

"I think I heard 'baout his havin' a fortin left him at the time, but I thought it was f'om a cousin down in South America," Jed went on, looking inquiringly at Sam.

"Heh, heh! thet was another time," said Sam, with his dry little laugh. "Good nation! ef all the luck thet 's threatened to hit him hed *done* it, he 'd be the richest man in this caounty. I tell ye, good luck 's allers a-sniffin' at his heels, but he don't never git bit. This time he got a letter f'om his cousin, tellin' him he 'd allers felt sorry he hed sech poor luck, an' he 'd made him sole heir of his estate, prob'ly wuth a couple o' thousand dollars. He hed some oncurable disease, he wrote, an' the doctors did n't give him over three months to live—"

"S'pose he lived forever," put in Jed, chuckling.

"No, sir; he died in good shape, an' in fac' he bettered his word, for he did n't live two months f'om the time he wrote to Seth; but I 'm blessed ef they did n't find there was some claim against the estate thet et it all up. Well, sir, I never saw any one laugh so hard ez Seth when he heard the news. It struck him ez a dretful good joke."

"He must hev a purty paowerful sense of the ridikerlus," said Jed, dryly.

"Well, he hez," assented Sam, rubbing his knees with his horny hands. "Ain't no better comp'ny 'an Seth. Ain't never daownhearted."

After a moment's silence Silas smiled, and, closing his eyes, pinched them between thumb and forefinger as if calling up some pleasing recollection. At last he said: "Ye know, Seth allers works by the day. He gin'ally has enough to do to keep him busy, an' allers doos his work up slick, but he never hed stiddy employment, on'y once, an' then it lasted on'y

one day. 'Member that, Sam? Time he
went to work at the Nutmeg State clock-
shop?"

" *Yes*, yes," laughed Sam, driving a
loose nail into the platform with his heel.

"Stiddy employment fer a day, eh?"
said Jed, grinning. "Thet 's 'baout ez
stiddy ez my hired man, an' he ain't stiddy
at all."

"It was this way," Silas went on.
"Seth allers was purty slick at han'lin'
tools, an' Zenas Jordan was foreman of the
shop, an' he offered Seth a place there at
twelve dollars a week, which was purty
good pay an' more 'n Seth could make
outside, 'thout it was hayin'-time. I met
him on his way to work fust mornin'.
'Well, luck 's with you this time, Seth,'
says I. 'Sh!' says he. 'Don't say thet,
or I 'll lose my job sure. It 's jes better 'n
nothin', thet 's all. *Don't* call it good
luck'; an' he laafed an' went along
a-whistlin'. B' Gosht! ef the blamed ol'
shop did n't burn daown thet very night,
an', ez ye know, they never rebuilt. Seth
he come to me nex' day, an' he says,

kinder reproachful: 'You 'd orter held yer tongue, Silas. I 'd be'n hopin' thet was a stroke er luck thet hed hit me by mistake, an' I was n't goin' to whisper its name for fear it 'd reckernize me an' leave me, and you hed to go an' yell it aout when ye met me.'" And Silas laughed heartily at recollection of the whimsicality.

"Cur'us, ain't it, what a grudge luck doos hev against some men?" remarked Jed, rubbing his smooth chin meditatively.

Far down the valley I heard the faint whistle of a locomotive.

"Las' story they tell 'baout Seth 's this," Silas said, rising and stretching himself, and then leaning against the wall of the station. " He 's a very good judge o' poultry, an', in fac', he gin'ally judges at the caounty fair every fall. Well, a man daown in Ansony told him he 'd pay him ten dollars apiece for a couple of fine thoroughbred Plymouth Rock roosters. Seth knowed a man daown Smithfield way named Jones thet owned some full-blooded stock, but ez he on'y kep' 'em fer home use he did n't set a fancy price on

'em, an' Seth knowed he could git 'em fer
seventy-five cents or a dollar apiece.
Well, it happened a day or two later he
was engaged to do a day's work fer this
man Jones, an' he went daown there. He
see two all-fired fine roosters a-struttin'
raound the place, an' he cal'lated to buy
them; but fer some reason he did n't say
nothin' 'baout it jes then to Jones, but
went to work at choppin' or sawin' or
whatever it was he was doin'."

"Said nothin', did he? *Must* ha'
sawed wood, then," interrupted Jed, looking over at me and winking.

"Sure! Well, when it kem time fer dinner he hed got up a good appetite, an' he
was glad to set daown to table, fer Jones
is a purty good feeder an' likes to see
people hev enough. Hed stewed chicken
fer dinner, an' Seth says he never enjoyed
any so much in his life. After dinner he
says, ' By the way, Jones, what 'll ye take
fer those two Plymouth Rock roosters 't
I saw this mornin'?' Jones bust aout
a-laafin', an' he says, ' Ye kin take what 's
left on 'em home in a basket an' welcome!'

Blamed ef Seth hed n't be'n eatin' a dinner that cost him nigh on to twenty dollars."

"Thet *must* hev riled him some," re-marked Jed.

"No, sir; he never seemed to realize the sitooation."

XXXII

CUPID ON RUNNERS

ITTLEWOOD PHILLIPS had been in love with Mildred Farrington for two years, ever since he first met her at the Hollowells' card-party. He had no good reason to doubt that his love was returned, yet so fearful was he that he had misread her feelings that he had never hinted that she was more to him than any of the girls he met at the church sociables and card-parties in Newington.

So matters stood when a snowfall that brought sleighing in its wake visited Newington, and Littlewood became conscious of the fact that he had actually asked Miss Farrington to take a ride with him. Of

173

course he must perforce bring matters to a crisis now.

The evening was soon at hand. A crescent moon shone in the west, and the stars were cold and scintillating. He walked to the livery-stable and asked for the cutter, and a few moments later he was driving a handsome chestnut to the house where his thought spent most of the time.

Miss Farrington kept him waiting a good half-hour, but he reflected that it was the privilege of her glorious sex, and it only made him love her the more. If she had come out and placed her dainty foot upon his neck he would have been overcome with rapture.

It was cold waiting, so he got out and hitched his horse and paced in front of her house, her faithful sentinel until death—if need be. Not that there was any reason to think that his services would be required, but it pleased his self-love to imagine himself dying for this lovely being of whom his tongue stood in such awe that it could scarce loose itself in her presence.

At last she appears. The restive horse
slants his ears at her and paws the ground
in admiration of her beauty, for Mildred
was as pretty as regular features, a fair
skin, and melting eyes could make her.

Littlewood handed her into the sleigh,
stepped in himself, tucked in the robes,
and chirruped to the horse.

That intelligent animal did not move.
A flush of mortification overspread the
face of the would-be amorous swain. A
balky horse, and at the start! What
chance would he have to deliver his precious message that was to make two hearts
happy? He clicked again to the horse,
but again the horse continued to stand
still.

"You might unhitch him, Mr. Phillips.
That would help," said Mildred, in her
sweet voice.

"Oh, yes—t-to be sure! I must have
tied him. I mean I—er—I di—I think I
did hitch—er—"

"There seems to have been a hitch
somewhere," she answered.

He stepped out of the sleigh and looked

over his shoulder at her in a startled way.
Could she mean anything? Was this
encouragement? Oh, no! It was too
soon. (Too soon, and he had been in love
two years!) He unhitched the horse and
once more placed himself beside his loved
one.

The frosty night seemed to have set a
seal upon her lips, for as they sped over
the crunching snow and left the town behind them she was silent.

" I must have offended her. I 've probably made a break of some kind," said
Littlewood to himself. " How unfortu-
nate! But I must tell her to-night. It is
now or never. She knows I never took
anybody but my mother sleigh-riding
before."

Then began a process of nerving himself
to the avowal. He ground his knees together until the bones ached. His breath-
ing was feverish.

Finally he made bold to say: " Mildewed." And then he stopped. He had
never called her Mildred before. He had

never called her Mildewed either, but that was accidental, and he hoped that she had not noticed the slip.

"I have something of the

greatest importance to say to you."

Did he imagine it, or did she nestle closer to him? He must have been mistaken, and to show that he was quite sure he edged away from her as

much as the somewhat narrow confines of
the sleigh would allow.

"What do you wish to say, Mr.
Phillips?"

"Mr." Phillips! Ah, then she was
offended. To be sure, she had always
called him that, but after his last remark
it must have an added significance.

"I—er—do you like sleigh-riding?"

"Why, of course, or else I should n't
have come."

Did she mean that as a slap at him?
Was it only for the ride, and not for his
company, that she had come? Oh, he
could never make an avowal of love after
that! He knew his place. This beautiful
girl was not for a faint-hearted caitiff like
himself.

"Nun—nun—no, to be sure not. I—
er—thought that was why you came."

Mildred turned her gazelle-like eyes
upon him. "I 'm afraid I don't understand you."

That settled it. If she did n't understand him when he talked of nothing in
particular, he must be very blind in his

utterance, and he could never trust his tongue to carry such a heavy freight as a declaration of love. No, there was nothing to do but postpone it.

Mildred drank in the beauty of the scenes, and wished that it were decorous for women to propose.

Under the influence of sweet surroundings, Mildred at last said pointedly: "Is it so that more people get engaged in winter than in summer?"

She blushed as she spoke. It was unmaidenly, but he was such a dear gump. Now he would declare himself. But she did not know the capabilities for self-repression of her two-year admirer.

He said to himself: "What a slip! What a delightful slip! If I were unprincipled I would take advantage of it and propose, but I would bitterly reproach myself forever, whatever her answer was."

So he said in as matter-of-fact tone as he could master when his heart was beating his ribs like a frightened cageling: "I really can't answer offhand, but I 'll look it up for you."

"Do. Write a letter to the newspaper.":

Her tones were as musical as ever, but
Littlewood thought he detected a sarcastic
ring in them, and he thanked his stars
that he had not yielded to his natural desire to propose at such an inauspicious
time.

"What was that important thing you
wanted to say?" asked Miss Farrington,
after several minutes of silence, save for
the hoofs and the runners and the bells.

"Oh, it wasn't of any importance!   I
mean it will keep. I—er—I was thinking
of something else."

"I think you have gone far enough,"
said she, innocently, looking over her
shoulder in the direction of home. Maybe
the return would loosen his obdurate
tongue.

His heart stopped beating and lay a
leaden thing in his breast.   Had he, then,
gone too far?   What had he said?   Oh,
why had he come out with this lovely being, the mere sight of whom was enough
to make one cast all restraint to the winds

and declare in thunderous tones that he loved her?

"I think that we 'd better go back," he said, and turned so quickly that he nearly upset the sleigh. "Your mother will be anxious."

"Yes; when one is accountable to one's mother one has to remember time. I suppose it is different when one is accountable to a—"

"Father?" said Littlewood, asininely.

"No; that was n't the word I wanted."

"A-a-aunt?"

Could Mildred love him if he gave many more such proofs of being an abject idiot?

"No; husband is what I want."

Littlewood's brain swam. He had been tempted once too often. This naïve girl had innocently played into his hands, and now the Rubicon must be crossed, even if its angry waters engulfed him.

"Pardon me, Miss—er—Mildred,"—he did not say Mildewed this time,—"if I twist your words into another meaning, but if you—er—want a husband—do you think I would do ?"

12*

A head nestled on his shoulder, a little hand was in his, and when he passed the Farrington mansion neither he nor she knew it.

XXXIII

MY TRUTHFUL BURGLAR

**I** HAD an experience with a burglar night before last. My family are all away, and I have been living alone in the house, a detached villa in New Jersey, for upward of a month. Several burglaries have occurred in the vicinity.

Night before last I was awakened about four o'clock by a noise made by a clicking door, and opening my eyes, I saw a smooth-faced, determined-looking man at my bedside. I did not cry out, nor hide under the bedclothes, nor do any of the conventional things that one does when a burglar comes to him.

I looked at him calmly for a moment, and then I said, "How d' do?"

An expression of surprise passed over

his intelligent features, but he said me-
chanically, " Pretty well, thank you.   And
you?"

"Oh, I 'm as well as could be expected
under the circumstances.   Are you the
burglar who has been doing this village?"

"I am," said he, drawing up a chair
and sitting down.

"Why don't you deny it?" I asked.   I
was n't afraid.   He amused me, this non-
chalant burglar.

"Well, because I 'm not ashamed of
my profession, for one reason, and mainly
because I was brought up by my father to
tell the truth."

"You tell the truth, and yet you are a
burglar.   How can you reconcile those
facts?"

"They are not irreconcilable," said he,
taking a corn-cob pipe out of his pocket
and filling it.   "I am a burglar, and my
father was one before me, but he was a
perfectly honorable man.   He never lied,
and I never lie.   I steal because that is
my profession, but I make it a rule to tell
the truth upon all occasions.   Why, if the

success of my venture to-night depended
upon my lying to you, I 'd immediately
leave this place, as innocent of plunder as
when I came in.   Where 's the silver?"

"Top drawer of the sideboard."   There
was a magnetism, a bonhomie, about the
man that captivated me.

"Are you armed?" asked he, as he
puffed at his pipe.

"If I had been I 'd have winged you
before this," said I, laughing.

"I believe you, and I honor you for being perfectly frank with me."

"Why, as to that, I 'm not to be out-
done in frankness by a thief."

"That will make my task so much the
easier.   After I 've finished this pipe I
want you to give me your word that
you 'll lie still until I 've taken all I want."

I admired the man's nerve, and I said:
"For the time being I consider you my
guest, and, Spanish fashion, my house is
at your disposal."

"Don't put it on that basis, or I will
leave at once.   This is no time for aping
the Spanish."

"You are right.   But I tell you candidly that I would far rather have found out that you were a liar than a burglar. Your lies would not be likely to injure me, but I 'll be out just so much by what you take.   I 'd much rather you were a liar."

"And I would not.   If I steal, I do but take something that, to paraphrase Shakspere, was yours, is mine, and has been slave to thousands; but to lie would

be to 'lay perjury to my soul,' and that I would not do, 'no, not for Venice'! "

"I see you know Shakspere," said I, punching my pillow so that I could be more comfortable.   I was reading this odd fellow, and I believed that I could dissuade him from his purpose.

"Know Shakspere? I was an actor once."

I felt that I had him, for I know actors better than he knew Shakspere.

"Did you ever play Hamlet?" I asked, sitting up in bed.

"I did; and I made such a hit that if it had n't been for the venality of the press and my sense of honor, I would have been adjudged one of the greatest Hamlets of the day."

"Give me the soliloquy. I give you my word that ordinarily I 'd rather be robbed than hear it, but I like your voice and I believe that you can do it justice."

A self-satisfied smile illuminated his face. He laid down the pipe and gave me the soliloquy, and it was n't bad.

"Bully!" I said, when he had finished. "Why, man, you make an indifferent thief, else you would have decamped long ago; but the stage has lost an actor that would have in time compelled the unwilling admiration of the press."

And so I jollied him, and he gave me the trial scene from "The Merchant of

Venice," and other selections, until dawn began to show in the east, when he picked up his bag and said, " It would be a shame to rob a white man like you."   Then he bade me good-by and left.

And I congratulated myself upon my knowledge of human nature, until I began to dress, when I found that the fellow had finished his burgling before I woke, and he has all my silver.

XXXIV

THE MAN WITHOUT A WATCH

HOMAS MORLEY knew the value of promptitude. He was a young man on whom ninety-two seasons had poured benefits and adversities, although many of the latter he took to be the former, his temperament shedding sorrow as a duck does water, to use a castanean simile.

He was a born and bred New-Yorker, but at the time of which we write he had been living for the last ten or twelve months in Uxton, up among the hills of northwestern Connecticut, studying the natives; for he was a writer.

Having filled a portfolio with material for enough dialect stories to run one of the great magazines for a year, he determined to seek his matter in the metropolis, and to that end applied for a reportership on the New York "Courier-Journal," in which paper many of his brightest things had appeared at remunerative rates.

As has been said, he knew the value of promptitude, so when, at eight o'clock one night, Farmer Phelps's hired man handed him a letter from James Fitzgerald, managing editor of the "Courier-Journal," asking him to come and see him in regard to a reportership as soon as possible, he made up his mind to take the train which left Winsonia, four miles distant, at six o'clock next morning. This would enable him to reach the office by half-past ten, and probably catch Mr. Fitzgerald on his arrival at his desk.

Next morning he arose at four, and when he left the house he had sixty minutes in which to walk four miles downhill — ample time, surely.

It was so ample that he would have had fifteen minutes to spare if the home clock had been right. As it was, he arrived at the station in time to see the train rapidly disappearing around a curve, on its way to New York. He laughed good-naturedly with the baggageman, and asked him when the next down train was due.

"Seven-thirty, sharp. You 'll not have to wait long."

Seven-thirty. That would bring him into the presence of Mr. Fitzgerald at just about the time he arrived at his sanctum. "Better than to have to wait in a presumably stuffy room," said he to himself, philosophically. He lit a cigar, and, as the air was bracing and he was fond of walking, he struck out into a five-mile-an-hour gait down the main street of Winsonia.

His footsteps led him farther than he had intended going, and when he reached the Baptist church at East Winsonia, he saw by its clock that it lacked but forty minutes of train-time, and he had four miles to make. He threw away the stump of his cigar, which had been out for some time, broke into a jog-trot, and, after covering a mile, he caught his second wind and mended his pace.

His fleetness would have served its turn
had not a malicious breeze blown his hat
over a high iron fence that surrounded a
churchyard.   By the time he had climbed
the fence and recovered his hat he had
consumed so many precious minutes that,
although he sprinted the last mile, he arrived at the station only in time to see
train No. 2 disappearing around that hateful curve.

The baggageman was standing on the
platform, and he said :

" Ain't once enough ? "

" More than enough for most people,"
said Thomas, whose rare good nature was
proof against even such a remark at such
a time.

The next train for New York was
due at nine fifty-six.   Being somewhat
blown, he walked around the corner to
a billiard-room, meaning to sit down
and watch whatever game might be in
progress.

" It may be," soliloquized Thomas,
" that Fitzgerald won't reach the office
until after lunch, and I 'll get there at

half-past two, in time to see him when he 's
feeling good."

He met Ned Halloway at the billiard-
room, and when Ned asked him to take a
cue he consented. Billiards was a game
in which he was apt to lose—himself, at
any rate; yet to-day his mind was enough
on the alert to enable him, after a time, to
glance at the clock over the bar in the next
room. It was forty-five minutes past
eight.

They began another game. Later he
looked again at the clock. A quarter of
nine. After another game he looked up
once more. "Fifteen minutes to ni—.
Say, Ned, what 's the matter with that
clock?" Ned looked at it, then at his
watch. "Why, it 's stopped!"

"You settle—see you later." And
Thomas was gone like a shot.

This time he had the rare pleasure of
noting how the rear car of a train grows
rapidly smaller as it recedes. In a moment the train disappeared around the
curve before mentioned.

"Say, Mr. Morley, you 've time to miss

13

the next, easy," said the baggageman, dryly.

Thomas was vexed, but he said pleasantly : "When is it due?"

"Half-past two. Better wait here and make sure of it."

"Oh, dry up! No; do the other thing; it 's on me."

After this little duty had been performed, Thomas, with an irrelevancy of action that might have struck an observer as amusing, made his way to the Y. M. C. A. rooms to read the magazines.

"Let 's see," said he; "I 'll get to his desk at seven. He 'll be hard at work, and, if he engages me, he may send me out on an assignment at once. Glad I missed the other trains."

Thus was Thomas wont to soliloquize. At one o'clock he went to Conley's Inn, and sat down to one of those dinners that attract drummers to a hotel. Necessarily, then, it was a good dinner, and one over which he lingered until nearly two. Then he went into the office and sat down.

The room was warm, and his dinner had made him drowsy. He decided to take a little nap. He had the faculty of waking when he pleased, and he willed to do so at fifteen minutes past two. It would be weakness for him to get to the station with too much time to spare, but this would give him a quarter-hour in which to go a half-mile.

His awakening faculty would seem to have been slightly out of order that day, however, and he did not arouse until twenty-nine minutes past two by the hotel clock.

Of course he did not make a fool of himself by trying to do a half-mile in sixty seconds; but he walked leisurely toward the station, intending to get his ticket and have that off his mind.

He laughed heartily at a corpulent fellow who darted by him, carrying a grip.

His laughter ceased, however, when, on turning the corner, he discerned the aforesaid fat man in the act of being assisted on to the platform of the last car by the brakeman, the train having acquired considerable momentum. Then he saw it disappear around a curve which was part of the road at that point. There were three explanations possible: either the train was behind time, or else his awakening faculty was in good repair, or the hotel clock was fourteen minutes fast. The latter proved to be the correct explanation of the somewhat vexing occurrence.

"Say, that 's a bad habit you have of missing trains," said his friend the baggageman. "Goin' to miss another—or do anything else?"

" No," said Thomas, shortly.

He knew that the next train at five was the last. This would make it possible to reach Fitzgerald at half-past nine. " Right in the heat of the work. He 'll engage me to get rid of me," laughed Thomas to himself. Then he continued: " I never heard of a man missing every train in a day, so I 'll risk calling on Laura before the next one starts."

Miss Sedgwick, the one he called Laura, lived out of town near the railroad track, and two miles nearer New York than Winsonia station.

She was a captivating girl, and when Thomas was in her presence he never took heed of time. He was lucky enough to find her at home. She seemed glad to see him, and was much interested in his account of how near he had come to catching some trains that day; and as nothing is so engaging as a good listener, the minutes passed on pneumatic tires. When at last he took note of the hour, it was five o'clock.

" That clock is n't right, is it?"

13*

"Yes, sir. Father keeps it at railroad time. Mercy! you 've lost your train again, have n't you?"

"Laura, this time it 's bad. I won't see him to-day, now, and to-morrow may not do. Let me go and kick myself."

"I 'm awfully sorry, Tom. I hope to-morrow won't be too late."

Thomas squeezed her hand and left her, feeling rather blue.

The railroad track was but a block away, and he walked over to it, not with suicidal intent, but just that he might tantalize himself with a view of the train as it sped by, which it should do in about a minute.

"At any rate," said he, "it won't be going around that dreadful curve."

It was the last of December, and the sun had set. When he reached the track he saw, far away, a glimmer of the head-light of the five-o'clock express.

Nearer and nearer it came. A moment more and it would rush by like a meteor. But it did n't. It slackened up at the very corner on which Thomas stood, to allow an official of the road to jump off.

Thomas was not slow, if he did miss trains now and then.   He swung himself on to the smoker.

"Go'n' far?" asked the brakeman.

"To New York," was his reply.

"You 're in luck."

"Well, I 've not missed more than three or four trains in my life!" said Thomas; and it was strictly true.

Half-past nine to the minute found him outside of the editorial rooms of the "Courier-Journal."

"Can I see Mr. Fitzgerald?" he asked of a boy who came in response to a knock.

"No, sir; he went out of town yesterday.   Be back to-morrow at twelve."

"DID you get my letter already?" asked Mr. Fitzgerald of Thomas Morley, when he came to his desk next morning and found that young man waiting for him.

"Yes, sir; and here I am."

"Well, sir, I like your promptness, and I 'll give you the place of a man whom we had to discharge for being too slow.   You seem to have what a reporter needs most of all—the 'get there' quality."

"I did n't allow any trains to pass me," said Thomas, modestly.

XXXV

THE WRECK OF THE "CATAPULT"

BY CL–RK R–SS–LL

The sea, the sea, the open sea,
The blue, the fresh, the ever free.
BARRY CORNWALL.

IF there be those who love not the sea, with its storms, its seaweed, its sharks and shrimps and ships, this is not the story for them, and they would best weigh anchor and steer for some tale written by a landlubber and full of green meadows and trees and such tommy-rot, for this is to be chock-a-block with nautical phrases.

And who am I, you ask? I am Joseph

Inland, the tenth of that name. We have always lived and died here in Birmingham, and followed the trade of cutlers; but when I was a babe of one year father told mother 't was time one member of the family followed the sea, wherever it went, and that he intended to make a sailor of me.

So before I was six I had heard of sloops and ferry-boats and belaying-pins and admirals and salt-junk, and longed to hear the wind whistling through the main-topgallantmast, and could say "boat-swain" as glibly as any sailor afloat. But father was in moderate circumstances; and so, much as he would have liked to, he could not afford to send me to sea when I was a boy, and that is why my one-and-twentieth birthday came and went and I had never been farther from Birmingham than my legs could carry me in a day; but you may be sure that I subscribed to the "Seaman's Daily," and through a friend who knew a sailor I had picked up such terms as "amidships," "deck," "boom," "bilge-water," "forecastle," and

the like, so that I was a seaman in everything save actual experience.

And in the amateur dramatic society of
which I was a member I always played
sailors' parts, and did them so well
that when we played "Hamlet" they
changed the part of the grave-digger to
that of a sailor for me, and I made a great
hit in it. The one who played Hamlet
did n't like the change, as it interfered
with his lines and his business with a skull,
and he refused to come on at all in that
act; but I sang a sea-song instead, and
the newspaper came out and said that
my singing was no worse than his acting
would have been, which I thought pretty
neat.

But enough of that. I was always fond
of joking, and had nigh unto a score of
comical sayings that I used to repeat to
my friends when they would come to our
house of an evening; but they did n't
often come. My father said I was as
comical a lad as he ever knew, and would
slap me on the back and roar that it was
the funniest thing he had heard in a

twelvemonth when I made one particular joke, the tenor of which I forget now. But all the jokes dealt with the sea.

Well, so much for my life up to my one-and-twentieth birthday. You have learned that if ever a body was fitted for a sea life, that body was mine.

By the time I was six-and-twenty I don't believe there was a sea term that I did not have at my tongue's end, and I always wore my trousers wide at the lower end, and kept a chew of tobacco in my mouth day and night, although after a time I failed to notice any taste in it.

It was a gladsome sight to see me go rolling to my work in the cutler's shop (for I still followed the old trade), with a hearty "Ho, landsman! good mornin' to ye!" to all I met, in true sailor fashion.

Our fare at home consisted of loblolly, ship's-biscuit, salt-junk, and plum-duff, with water drawn from casks. My dear old mother used sometimes to wish for home-made bread and fresh meat and vegetables and pump water; and I remember, one winter, brother died of the scurvy;

but I was better content than if he had
died of some landsman's complaint, and

mother was glad to put up with anything,
she was so proud that I was to be a seaman.

I had a carpenter construct my parents' bedroom so that the whole floor could be rocked; and on stormy nights I would stay up and by a simple mechanism keep it a-rocking until poor old mother would be as sick as if she were in the Channel. But I never heard her murmur. *She* was fit for a sailor's wife.

On such nights father never went to bed, but stayed down-stairs. There was little of the seaman's spirit in the old man.

When I was one-and-thirty I had a rare chance to ship before the mast on a whaler sailing from Liverpool; but as business was pretty brisk at the shop, I decided to wait, and the offer was not renewed when she returned, three years later.

When I was forty dear mother entered her last port. The doctor, a blundering landlubber, fond of landsmen's phrases, said she died of insufficient nutriment. Be that as it may or what it may, in her I lost one whose heart was always on my going to sea. Douse my top-lights if ever there was a craft that carried a stancher heart from barnacle to binnacle than did the old lady, and I had her buried in shrouds, with a cannon-ball at the foot of the coffin, as befitted the mother of one who was going to be a seaman.

After she died I became even more impatient to be off to sea, for there 's no air so pure as the sea air, no hearts so true as seamen's hearts, no weed like seaweed, and no water that 's fit to drink save sea water; but business was pretty good, so, for the present, I decided to stay ashore; but I always read the shipping news with as much keenness as any sailor afloat.

AND now I 've come to the end of my yarn. I named it "The Wreck of the 'Catapult'" because it had a salty savor. It was the name of one of my favorite Sunday-school books when I was a lad. Now I am an old man, threescore and ten, and have been alone in the world a score of years. Heaven denied me the blessing of children, but I have a grandson who is as hot for the sea as I was.

Ah, me! Next week I am going to apply for admission to the Sailors' Home;

for although circumstances have prevented my ever seeing the ocean or scenting its salty breezes, I have always been, and always shall be, at heart a British seaman.

Shiver my timbers!

ESSAYS AT ESSAYS

XXXVI

THE BULL, THE GIRL, AND THE RED SHAWL

THERE is no incident in all the realms of literature, from the "penny dreadful" up to the three-volume novel, that has afforded so much material for the pen of the writer of fiction as the delightful episode of the bull, the young girl with the red shawl, and the young girl's lover. Sometimes the cast includes the lover's hated rival, but the story may be told without using him.

It is thirty-odd years since I first came across this thrilling adventure in the pages of a child's book, very popular at the time. How well I remember how my young blood—to be exact, my seven-year-old blood—thrilled as I mentally watched this frail girl, with a start of just three feet, lead the tremendous and horribly savage bull in a three-hundred-yard sprint, only to trip at last on the only obstruction in the ten-acre field; how, just as the bull reached her, she flung her red shawl a few rods to the right; how the bull, leaving her, plunged after it; how she, weak and trembling, ran to the stone wall and managed to vault it just as her lover, a brawny blacksmith, who had seen the whole affair at too great a distance to be of immediate service, reached the wall and received her in his arms. "Oh, Kenston," she murmured, "you have saved my life!" And then she fainted, and I believe the bull ate up the shawl; at any rate, its part in that particular story was ended.

I have always felt that, thrilling as this scene was, it had not been worked for all it was worth; but an extensive reading since then has brought me to the conclusion that, first and last, it has been worked for its full value.

The next time that I read the enthralling narrative I was some years older, but the memory of the other telling was still fresh within me; and so, when, in the second chapter, I read about a savage old bull, one Hector, the property of Squire Flint, the meanest man in the county,—not that his meanness had anything to do with the story, but it is one of the conventions that a savage bull shall be owned by a cross, crabbed, and thoroughly stingy man,—I say, when I had read thus far my pulse quickened. Inexperienced as I was, I somehow sensed the coming situation. I seemed to know as by clairvoyance that, however limited the heroine's wardrobe might be in some respects, there was one article of apparel that she surely possessed, or would possess in time to meet the exigencies. True enough, in the very next chapter her maiden aunt, a saintly old lady of ninety, died and bequeathed to her sorrowing niece a red pongee shawl of great value—as a bull-enrager. The book had seemed prosy at the start, but now that

14*

I knew what was coming, and that it was *that* that was coming, I read on breathlessly.

Needless to say that in the next chapter the young girl fell in love with a strapping young fellow, who immediately proposed  that they take a walk. How well I knew, though they did not, where that walk would lead them! The mad bull—in this case it was mad, although any old bull will do, mad or not— was rampant in a lot a mile south of the young girl's house, and they started to walk due north; but I knew full well that they would need to cross that particular pasture before they got home, and a few pages later found them climbing over a stone wall into the bull's domain, and then they walked along, intent only on their new-found happiness.

The day was chilly,—in the middle of a particularly hot July,—so that the girl could have an excuse to wear her red shawl. Now, having brought two of the actors upon the stage, the cue was soon given to the bull; and in a moment the happy lovers, feeling the ground tremble beneath their feet, turned and saw Hector, his horns gyrating with rage, his eyes bulging out, and his head lowered as he thundered along straight for the pongee bequest. To take her under his strong arm and to rush forward were the only things for the young man to do, and he did them; and then the rest ran as per schedule. I believe that in this case the young man threw the girl into a tree and then plunged down a woodchuck's hole. At any rate, the girl was unharmed. That is the one unalterable formula in constructing these bull stories: save the girl unharmed. You may break the young man's leg or arm, and you may do what you will with the bull, but the young girl must come through unscathed.

It was years before this moving incident ceased to hold me, and in that time

how many changes were rung on it!   Once
only was the red shawl absent, and I wondered how in the world the bull was to be
infuriated, as he was a singularly mild
beast in the earlier chapters, and on May-
days had been festooned with garlands.
Then, too, the girl was in deep mourning
—for her lover!   But the ten-acre lot was
all right, and as the author was a clever
man, I felt that he would find a way to
run the act with a small cast and no prop-
erties.   So I read on, and after wondering,
together with the girl herself, what could
have caused the peaceful old bovine to
chase her, tail up and head down, the full
length of a particularly long pasture, she
and I found out when she realized that,
the day being sunny, she had picked up
her cousin's parasol, which was necessarily
of a brilliant scarlet.   She had no lover,
for, as I say, he had died—two chapters
before the book was begun; but she did
have presence of mind, and so she inserted
the point of the parasol in the bull's
mouth, and then opened it, and while he
was extracting it with his fore paws, she

reached the fence and vaulted it in the usual way.

The possibilities of the incident are by no means exhausted, and so far from "Amos Judd" being the last story in which it was used, I saw it in a tale published this month, and this time with the full paraphernalia of hated rival, lover, red shawl, and all; but for me it had lost its zest. To be sure, if they would make the hero an athlete, and have him bravely stand his ground while the girl climbed to the top of an enormous elm, and then, just as the bull lowered his head to toss him, have the hero jump high in the air and make the bull pass beneath him, and as he reached ground again seize the bull, not by the horns, but by the tail, and, swinging it three times around his head, dash it against a tree and stun it,—that is, if its tail were securely welded to its body, —there would be an original treatment of the subject. And if its tail were but loosely fixed to it, the hero could pull it out, and the bull, filled with chagrin, would walk off, dismayed and humiliated.

But, pending that form of the story, I am studiously avoiding all novels that contain heroines with red shawls, or that make early reference to fierce bulls, or that speak of a certain ten-acre lot peculiarly adapted for lovers' peregrinations; for, like the successful burglar, I know the combination.

XXXVII

CONCERNING DISH-WASHING

HAS the reader ever considered how much time is wasted every day by busy women in the work of washing dishes? Of course, if a man has plenty of money and, from philanthropic motives, engages a girl to perform this unpleasant—I had almost said "duty"—this unpleasant task, I suppose we cannot, strictly speaking, regard her time as wasted, for she might else be loafing in an intelligence-office without gaining a scrap of that article. I refer to the lives led by weary housewives who, having no aid from a hired housemaid, day out and day in will make themselves thin by the never-ceasing and perfectly useless grind of dish-washing; for the dishes don't stay clean for more than a few hours.

For years I ate my meals in selfish content, little recking at what cost the clean service was gained, until I discovered that my sister, who is also my housekeeper, had sold her piano, not having time to play upon it. I was shocked to think what a power this custom of dish-washing had over the minds of the feminine portion of our public.

But this dreadful waste of time that is going on in thousands of homes in this country every day was brought home to me in a still more striking manner not long after. My sister went away to visit a friend, and left me to keep bachelor's hall. I had always had a good taste for cooking, although hitherto my practice had been confined to boiling eggs and buttering hot toast on a plate at the back of the stove. The first meal that I prepared, a breakfast, consisted of oatmeal, steak, fried potatoes, bread, butter, milk, and water. We will pass over the meal itself, as its discussion is foreign to our purpose. Indeed, the less said about it the better.   It was nine when I had finished eating, and dumped my dishes and knives and forks into tepid water.   I am a fast worker, but the clock in the neighboring church had ceased striking twelve when my last dish was wiped and put away.

I had hoped to do a little writing that morning, but it was now time to get luncheon.   Luckily, that meal called into play very few dishes, and by two, or half-past, I had made an end of my second stint.   Feeling elated that I had a whole afternoon on my hands, I prepared a course dinner.   I found some cold soup in the refrigerator, and I bought a bluefish, five or six pounds of beef for roasting, some Parker House rolls, and a lemon-pie for dessert.   There were lettuce and eggs in the house, and plenty of canned vegetables.   I also made some good coffee, with the aid of a French coffee-pot, that indispensable adjunct of a well-ordered household.   I found that the courses were very hard to manage so that they would follow in their proper order.   They were n't even satisfied to finish together like evenly matched racers, but the roast was burned five minutes before I thought of warming up the soup, and ten minutes before I had scaled the fish. Then the latter would n't broil readily until most of it was in the fire. The vegetables I forgot entirely, and I decided at the last moment to deny myself the salad, as dinner was waiting and I was hungry. I might add that I inadvertently cut the pie with the fish-knife, and that cast a damper on the dessert. However, as I said, the coffee was good—and, anyhow, I am digressing.

It was seven when I emptied my dishes into the water, and I worked with a will, as I had a very exciting novel that I was desirous of finishing. It was a few minutes past eleven when I emptied my dishpan for the last time, and then I was ripe for bed.

As time wore on I became more dexterous in the use of the dish-cloth and -towel, and the day before sister returned I devoted but six hours to dish-washing. To be sure, I had given up course dinners, because they took too many plates, and for other reasons that need not to be quoted here.

As I say, I am a fast worker, and yet it took me over six hours a day to clean the crockery. Assuming that a woman can do it in eight hours, she wastes half of her waking moments in drudgery beside which the making of bricks without straw would be a pastime.

There is absolutely nothing in the dish-washing habit to recommend it. It is ruinous to hands and temper, and, indeed, I do not see but that it is immoral.   Anything that puts us in the proper mood for swearing is immoral, and there is nothing in the whole housekeeping routine so conducive to highly spiced language as dish-washing.

And to what purpose is this waste of time?   I won't go so far as to advocate a return to the fingers that were used before forks for the purpose of conveying food to the mouth, for that would but relieve us from the washing of cutlery; but I will say that the man who will invent a cheap yet very ornate dinner service that may be destroyed after once using will have earned the undying gratitude of the women of this country and a princely fortune besides.

And when he has invented it, sister may go on another visit.

XXXVIII

A PERENNIAL FEVER

THE world hears much of the dangers of typhoid and yellow and scarlet fever, and the skill of physicians is ever employed to reduce those dangers to a minimum; but in every country, at all seasons of the year, there is a fever that numbers its victims by the thousand, and yet no doctor has ever prescribed for it, nor is there any drug in the pharmacopœia that will alleviate it.

The malady to which I refer is hen fever.

If a city woman intends marrying a city man, and then moving out a little way into the country, as she values her peace of mind, let her make sure that he is immune. Unless, indeed, both are prepared to come down with it at once. For it is unlike all other fevers in that a man and his wife may have it together and be happy; but if he or she have it alone, then woe be to that house.

The germs of hen fever are carried in a chance conversation, in a picture of gallinaceous activity, in the perusal of a poultry-book. A man hears or looks or reads, and the mischief is done. The subtle poison is in his blood, although he knows it not.

Hen fever takes various forms. With some it is manifested in a desire to keep a few blooded fowls and breed for points; with another, to keep a few birds for the sake of fresh eggs and broilers: but in whatsoever form it come, it will cause the upheaval of its victim's most cherished plans and habits.

He may have been an ardent admirer of Shakspere, and in the evenings it has been his wont to read aloud to his wife while she knitted; but now, little recking what she does, he reads to himself " Farm Poultry " or " The Care of Hens," or—and this is the second stage of the disease—he reads aloud to her that hens cannot thrive without plenty of gravel, that cracked wheat is better than whole corn for growing

pullets, that the best way to cure a hen of eating her own eggs is to fill one with mustard, etc.

Time was when he had an opinion on politics, on finance, on literature, on the thousand and one things that make for conversation, and his neighbors dropped in to hear him talk engagingly of what he had read or seen; but now, when they come, he tells them that his brown Leghorn hen laid twenty eggs in twenty-five days, while his buff Cochin laid only eight in the same time; that his white Plymouth Rock is crop-bound, and his Wyandotte rooster has the pip.

Lucky indeed is his wife if he stick to the good old way of hatching chickens by hens instead of kerosene-oil; for if he get an incubator she had better get a divorce. How many homes have been wrecked by patent incubators will never be known.

But even if the fevered one stick to the natural method of hatching, there will be many times when his wife will wonder why she left a comfortable and sociable home to spend her evenings alone; for he will be in the hen-house, setting hens, or washing soiled eggs, or divesting nestlings of the reluctant shell, or dusting his whole

flock with the snuff-like insecticide, or
kerosening their roosts.

With some the fever never abates; with
some it is intermittent; some have it hard-
est in the spring of the year, when hens
are laying their prettiest, and profits may
be figured in money as well as on paper.
But whether it be light or heavy, hen fever
will run its course without let or hindrance;
and, as I have hinted, happy is the wife
who comes down with it simultaneously
with her husband; for, though their neighbors will shun them as they would a
deadly pestilence, yet they will be company for each other, and will prate cease-
lessly, yet cheerily, upon the best foods
for laying hens, the best exposure for
coops, how many hens can live in one
house with best results, when a chicken
should be weaned of bread, what breed
of hens is least idiotic, and kindred
topics.

As for me, I am free to come and go
among hens; to look on their markings
with unmoved eye; to view their output

with normal pulse; to hear "the cock's shrill clarion" without pricking up my ears; to read of the latest thing in incubators without turning a hair: for I have survived the fever; I am an immune.

XXXIX

"AMICUS REDIVIVUS"

OSEPHUS says, "Post hoc ergo propter hoc," and it might well be applied to the concerns of this day, for what one of us has not at some time or other felt a "pactum illicitum," a "qualis ab incepto," as it were, permeating his whole being, and bringing vividly before the retina the transitory state of all things worldly? As Chaucer said:

> For who so wolde senge the cattes skin,
> Than wol the cat wel dwellen in here in.

For it cannot be gainsaid that, despite the tendency toward materialism, the cosmic rush and the spiritual captivity that lead so many brave souls into the martyrdom of Achiacharus, there is in all of us a certain quality that must and will assert itself.

It seems but yesterday that Shelley, in his poem on " Mutability," said:

We are as clouds that veil the midnight moon;

but how pat is the application to-day! We *are* as clouds. You who boast your-self of your ancestry, you whose dignity is as a cloak of ermine, ye are but clouds. How well Goethe knew this! We all re-member those lambent lines of his—I can-not translate adequately, so I will quote from the original German:

Fräulein Anna, das Papier in Deutschland ist wie das Papier in Amerika.

Ages ago Sophocles had worded it in almost the same phrase:

Oh, race of mortal men oppressed with care!
What nothings are we, like to shadows vain,
    Cumb'ring the ground and wandering to and fro.

The greatest poets, from Le Gallienne down to Shakspere, have been aware of this evanescent property in the cumbrous and exsufflicate prowlers amid these

" glimpses of the moon." Well may we say with Cæsar, " Quamdiu se bene gesserit."

There is always a touch of ozone in the words of Horace, and we find him saying of this very thing, " Precieuse ridicules pretiosa supel-lex." Could it have been said better? How airily he pricks the bubble of man's self-es-teem! "Dressed in a little brief authority," man plays his part amid mundane happenings tre-

melloid and sejant, and with a sort of in-nate connascence, a primitive conglutinate efflorescence, he approaches nearer and nearer, day by day, to that time when, as Shakspere hath it, " the beachy girdle of the ocean " will resolve itself into its com-ponent parts, and man as man will cease to exist.

15**

But, to pass to a more inchoate view of these things,—to the "opum furiata cupido" of the ancient Latins,—what is there in all this that tends to lessen a man's self-glorification, his auto-apotheosis?   Victor Hugo can tell us:

> Petit bourgeois père La Chaise
> Pour prendre congé tour de force
> Connaisseur tout Thérèse
> Façon de parler Edmund Gosse.

The author of "Les Misérables" was himself a man, and he knew.   And no less a man was Coplas de Manrique, and in his beautiful lyric, "Caballeros," he says:

> Tiene Vd.-Usted mi sombrero
> Tiene Vd.-Usted mi chaleco
> No lo tengo, no lo tengo
> Tiene Vd.-Usted mi.

"Noblesse oblige," and it behooves all of us, however mighty our positions in life, to unbend a little and try to mollify these manducable and irresoluble phases of molecular existence, to the end that we may accomplish a "vis medicatrix naturae" and a "vade mecum" that shall be valuable to us in our journey to the tomb and through nether space.

So, then, may we " with an unfaltering trust approach our grave," and, as Schiller says so musically :

Ich kann nicht mit der linken Hand schreiben.

XL

THE PROPER CARE OF FLIES

IT is a fact beyond cavil that ninety-
nine flies out of a hundred perish
every year for lack of proper
care on the part of housewives; that the
attention that is lavished upon the house-
cat, if expended upon the house-fly, would
cause him to stay with us throughout the
twelvemonth.

I have devoted years of patient study
to the busy buzzers, and I speak as one
having authority. Flies need warmth as
much as humans do—nay, more than their
biped brethren, for we can stand the early
autumn frosts without a fire, but it is those
few days that kill off the little fellows that
have been our winged companions through
the summer season, singing in the new

236

day, sampling our butter and meats, and tickling us half to death with their erratic pilgrimages and divagations. A little forethought on our part, a speedier lighting of the furnace fires, and flies in midwinter would no longer be a rarity.

This well-nigh universal carelessness is due to a woeful ignorance as to the habits of the fly, and not to intentional cruelty. Why, we know more about the ways of the wapiti than of the most common occupant of our houses. To give an instance, most people refer to the fly as a scavenger, a lover of tainted meats and vegetables. This is only because he is so often forced to eat tainted meat or go without altogether. There are fresh milk and fish for the cat, dainty titbits for the dog, millet and rape for the canary; yet how many Christian people think to provide something tempting for the flies? But too often we begrudge them the crumbs that fall from the table.

So far from flies loving " high " meat, it is an acquired taste with them. This had long been a theory with me, but it is only a year since I proved it by an interesting experiment. I secured a setting of flies' eggs,—not thoroughbred eggs, but just the ordinary barn-yard variety,—and I set them under a motherly bluebottle fly, after I had made her a comfortable nest in a pill-box. I saw to it that she had the proper food for a setting fly—not mush and milk, but flakes of hominy and grains of sugar once a day. I also dusted her nest thoroughly with insecticide and covered her with a tea-strainer so that she would be secure from molestation from other flies. For three weeks she was faithful to her duties, and then, one morning, I saw that she had experienced the sweet joys of motherhood, for there, on the edge of her nest, sat thirteen—mark the number—cunning little flies, pluming and preening themselves with innate skill. I could scarce keep back the tears.

For a few days I let the little flock follow their mother, and then I shut them up away from her in my guest-chamber and began their education. The sweetest milk was theirs from the start, and after a

week of bread diet, that their feathers
might be strengthened, I began to give
them small scraps of porter-house steak
and Southdown mutton.   It was wonder-

ful to see how the little beggars throve.
One night I slept in the guest-chamber,
and they awoke me before the robin's
matin song, although they were not three
weeks old.   Their tread had a firmness, a
titillating power, that never comes to a
tramp fly or to one improperly nurtured.
Then, their buzzing was so sonorous that
sleep was impossible once they tuned up,

so I was in no danger of becoming a drowse-abed.

When they were two months old I determined to test my theory. I procured some meat from the larder of a gormand friend of mine, and brought it into my guest-chamber in an air-tight box. Then I opened the box and awaited developments. If flies are natural-born birds of carrion, then they would rush upon this stuff with avidity. I hid behind the arras—if I am quite sure what arrases are—and watched my little pets with some concern. They flew over to the meat, sniffed it disdainfully, buzzed with ire for a few seconds, and then flew to the ceiling with every appearance of disgust. ' Then the largest one signaled to his fellows, and they flew down once more, lifted the " condemned beef " in their talons as firemen seize a life-preserving net, and sailed to the open window, where they dropped it. In five minutes' time it was black with flies that had not received proper nurture. Was I pleased? I was delighted. I set forth a feast of sugar on top of my bald head, and sat in the guest-chamber until my pets had made an end of eating.

The nineteenth century is nearing its close, and the house-fly is not a perfect insect; but, housekeeper, it lies with you to improve the breed. Exercise a little care in the choice of their food, and when the biting days of early fall come upon the land, make provision for warming your little guests of the summer days, and if the winds of winter whistle sharp they will be answered by the hot little buzz of myriads of flies.

www.ingramcontent.com/pod-product-compliance
Lightning Source LLC
Chambersburg PA
CBHW020055030726
47498CB00006B/1799